Also by Nora Everly

The Sweetbriar Mountain Series:

In My Heart

Heart Words

From the Heart

Heart to Heart

Change of Heart

Honeybrook Hollow:

Next to You

Make You Mine

By Your Side

Sweetbriar Short Stories:

Holiday Hearts

Conversation Hearts

Let It Snow

The Cozy Creek Collection:

Fall at Once

From Smartypants Romance:

Oh Brother!

Crime and Periodicals

Carpentry and Cocktails

Hotshot and Hospitality

Architecture and Artistry

Teachers' Lounge

Passing Notes

Star Crossed Lovers:

(*As Piper Everly, co-written with Piper Sheldon*):

<u>Midnight Clear</u>

Get exclusive sneak peeks of upcoming releases through Nora's newsletter and Facebook group, The Everly Afters.

Heart to Heart
The Sweetbriar Mountain Series

Nora Everly

For Jack and Emma

Chapter 1
Liam

There she was.

I hovered in the back of the long line for my daily hit of caffeine surreptitiously watching as she bustled around the espresso machine. I caught her eye and grinned as her cheeks turned red and she quickly looked away.

Violet's Café in Sweetbriar, Oregon, had become somewhat of a sanctuary for me since moving to town a few months back. The coffee was addicting, but that wasn't the main attraction anymore. Holly Barrett, the little sister of the owner, had caught my eye at first sight when she'd returned to town soon after I'd arrived, and I hadn't been able to look away ever since.

I refused to think about how many months I had been here or how long I'd been silently pining over the gorgeous blonde behind the counter. After my medical discharge from the Army, I vowed never to be bound by a clock or a schedule that I didn't create for myself ever again. My therapist's words floated through my mind as the line slowly moved through the shop.

To better spend your time, start by understanding where your time is spent.

Long line today or not, hopeless crush tearing up my heart or not, I liked it here. Time felt different here. Hours could pass and feel like nothing at all. Violet's coffee shop was heaven on earth, especially to someone who'd been stuck in a desert and bound by somebody else's rules for the last decade. The happy chaos of this place—not to mention the delicious smells, friendly faces, and homey feel—soothed me in a way I never wanted to lose. It was the polar opposite of the life I had known before I came to Sweetbriar.

Plus, as an entertaining bonus, this place had seen some *shit.* Town gossip, relationship dramas, jet-lagged travelers, ski-bums passing through on their way up the mountain, and the best part, the Barrett family themselves: boisterous, loving, and loud.

The line moved at a slow but steady pace. It was early afternoon, and Holly was the only barista behind the counter. It wasn't usually this busy at this time of day, but I didn't mind the wait, not when I had something as beautiful as her to look at.

"Finally," a deep voice boomed, and I tensed, ready to —what?

Nothing, stand down. He's probably harmless.

"I've been dying to see you all day, Holly." His tone turned flirty, and the muscles in my jaw ticked as I listened to him hit on her, ready to step in if he took it too far. Or maybe I'd step in anyway. She was obviously not interested and there was something about him I didn't like.

"Sorry for the wait." She brushed her hands down the front of her half-apron, ignoring his come-on as she faced him. "What can I get for you today, Jared?"

"So many things, babe. But we'll start with the usual, a cappuccino. And I'd like to add that date I've been asking about."

Between my teeth grinding together hard enough to hurt and the possessive rage blinding me as I watched him chat her up, I knew I was only kidding myself when it came to being *just friends* with Holly.

"I can't. I, um—" she murmured while stammering over her words and avoiding his eyes. She was sweet and I had the sense that hurting someone's feelings by saying "no" wasn't easy for her.

"So, listen." He barreled on, ignoring the not-so-subtle hints she was giving him. "I want your number, babe. I'll take you to dinner in the city, then maybe to a club? I remember how much you liked to dance back in high school."

"I—like I told you before, I'm not in the right head space for dating right now, okay? I have a lot going on. It's not you, it's a me thing. I need to get settled back in town, and I still—"

"Aw, come on. Any head space you're in is fine with me, and I bet I can settle you down." He reached across the counter and pulled her cell from the half apron tied around her waist. "I want your number."

"Jared!" Shocked, she jumped back, and I lurched forward, snatching the phone from his hand before he could get her number from it.

"Watch it. She said no." I passed it back to Holly, shoulder-checking him to the side as I stepped between him and the counter. She managed a tremulous smile as she mouthed, "Thank you," and took it, tucking it into her back pocket with a pointed glance toward a deliberately oblivious Jared.

"Oh really? She did?" Huffing a humorless laugh, he glared at me. "Because I didn't hear a '*no*'. I heard a 'not right now' or at the very least a 'maybe another time'. He turned back to her with a smarmy grin that I was *this close* to knocking off his face. "Sorry, babe. We'll make plans later." After stuffing a wad of cash in the tip jar, he took his order and stormed out.

I was last in line and despite the wait, the shop was fairly empty as most folks had taken their orders to go. A few customers lingered in the corner happily chatting. A quick glance showed they either hadn't noticed what had transpired or didn't want to intervene. "If I was out of line by stepping in—I mean, what he did is not okay, and if you'd wanted to tell him off yourself or maybe smack him around a little bit, I'm sorry—"

"Don't apologize. It's okay, I'm usually pretty good about taking care of myself. I wasn't expecting him to do anything like that. I've known him since kindergarten, he's always been pushy but harmless. Plus, I owe him for —it's a long, dumb, convoluted story but you might as well hear it from me. Basically, he saved me from making a huge mistake. My fiancé was a cheater and he let me know about it. Hence the Holly-left-a-guy-at-the-altar crap that sometimes goes around town about me, among other things." She stopped short in frustration. "I don't want to talk about Jared. *Gah*, I'm sorry, Liam. What'll it be?" she asked, as if she didn't tease me every day about ordering the same thing.

I smiled softly. "Why don't you surprise me this time?" I'd be keeping an eye on that prick. My protective hackles were up. But for now, I just wanted to make her feel better.

The heavy lashes that shadowed her freckled cheeks flew up in surprise. "Really?"

"Yeah, but nothing too sweet, I—"

Our eyes met. "Shh." Holding up a finger, she grinned. "I know what you'll like."

She didn't know even half of what I'd like from her.

My mouth turned up at the corner. "Okay, show me what you got."

She turned, reaching high on the shelf behind the counter for two glasses before filling them with ice. Stifling a groan, I watched her shirt rise up to bare a sliver of skin. I guess I was staying here for my coffee, and I didn't mind one bit.

Shoving my lust-fueled thoughts to the back of my mind, I forced myself to stop watching her gorgeous ass as she worked and raised my gaze. But it was useless when the sight was not only burned onto my retinas but also into my senses. I slammed my eyes shut as I forced the memory of having my hands on that ass out of my head.

We had kissed a few weeks back and it had been driving me to distraction ever since.

Violet threw a Valentine's Day party in the shop every year and for the latest one she'd come up with the bright idea to use balloons as a Valentine's version of Christmas mistletoe. Holly and I had found ourselves beneath a dozen or so and had made the most of it in the back room. It had happened in a rush of sensation and surprise and the feeling that I finally had somewhere to belong again, but it hadn't lasted.

"I'm not ready to jump into anything," she had said after. So I agreed to be her friend and held off asking her on a real date. We hadn't talked about it since. Deep down I knew I wasn't ready for anything serious either; I was still recovering from my time in the Army, among other things. The trouble was my heart didn't seem to agree with my head and logic went out the window whenever I got near her. The way my body jolted with electricity every time we got close made it glaringly obvious that I had feelings for her. But unlike Jared, the deluded dickhead who just left, I knew how to listen.

Just friends . . .

I let out a sigh, watching as she pulled a shot of espresso, then forced myself to stop remembering our kiss as she prepared my drink. I had to distract myself; the direction my thoughts were going in was treacherous.

"Taste this." She dropped a straw into the glass then slid it across the counter with a sexy wink. I almost groaned out loud. Friends didn't wink at each other, did they? Or at least they shouldn't. But maybe it was my lingering thoughts about our kiss that made the wink sexy, and she hadn't intended it to be. Damn, I was a mess over her.

I raised the glass to my lips, my eyebrows popping up as the flavor hit my tongue. "What is this?"

"It's sugar-free, so no worries." She waved a hand up and down in front of me. "I know how you like to keep things healthy." It was true, I was somewhat of a health nut. "But I've noticed your weekly cinnamon muffin indulgence, hence the drink. You like?"

"It tastes like when I dunk the muffin in my coffee, except it's iced. Delicious." I took another sip, nodding in appreciation.

"Exactly." One shoulder shrugged up as her pretty eyes sparkled with satisfaction. "For some reason, it's not as good hot. It's my favorite despite its healthy qualities. Normally I have the eating habits of a stoned raccoon at a full dumpster, but Vi was experimenting with healthier drink options last week and now I'm hooked." She placed a straw in her glass and took a sip for emphasis.

I chuckled. "Well, this might turn out to be my new favorite too. Sit with me?" I invited without thinking. "The rush is gone; you could take a break."

Her cute nose wrinkled up in uncertainty. "Do you really think we should?"

"What happened on Valentine's Day, stays on Valentine's Day. Right?" I cajoled with a grin.

"Right," she confirmed with a laugh. "Holiday hall pass."

"Yup." I gestured to the sofa in the corner then

headed that way. Heat surged through my veins when I heard her footsteps clicking over the wood floor behind me. "Besides, I think it's World Compliment Day. I heard it on the radio on the way to work this morning." I turned and gave her a wink of my own. "We should be okay to have coffee together. Holiday hall pass and all that . . ."

"Really? What a cute idea for a holiday." She sat on the brown leather armchair perpendicular to the couch. "Well, you look very handsome today, Liam. In honor of the holiday, of course."

I sat and held up my glass in her direction. "And you're as gorgeous as ever."

Obviously, it hadn't escaped my attention that she'd made two drinks when I asked her to sit with me. *Was taking a break with me her plan all along?*

I studied her face but, as usual, it was inscrutable. I decided not to question my good fortune and just enjoy her company. She was a fascinating mix of wide open, heart on her sleeve, friendliness, and hot-as-fuck innocent flirtation, and I was the fool dangling on her hook like a hapless fish with a semi-hopeless crush.

"Why, thank you, kind sir. Cheers to holidays and good friends." She tapped her glass to mine. "I should have grabbed some muffins or a cookie. Or would that have been overkill, Mr. Healthy?" she teased.

"No, not overkill. But it would've definitely spoiled my dinner." A blond curl escaped her loose ponytail when she laughed, and I wanted to tuck it behind her ear. I wanted to take that rubber band out and get my hands in her hair again. God, it was soft. It had felt like silk in my palms when we kissed.

I knew I should stop looking at her as though we stood a chance. As if I could ever be good for her with all my baggage, but I couldn't stop myself. She was like sunshine, and I was starved for more of her light.

"What's for dinner tonight? Do you cook? We never covered that topic on Valentine's Day."

"I can. I used to cook dinner with my mom every night until she, um . . ." *Died. Why did everything in my past have to be such a downer?*

"Liam . . ." Her voice was gentle as if she knew my history, and maybe she did. Her brother-in-law, Luke, was my best friend. I'd followed him to Sweetbriar after leaving the Army and he was the reason I was still here.

I shrugged, not wanting to bring her down. "Yeah, I'm not opposed to sweets, and I can cook pretty much everything. I'm just not quite at stoned-raccoon level."

Her knowing eyes held mine with that warmth and that light that I needed so badly in my life. "Well, I don't cook, as you know." Her mouth quirked up at the corner and she leaned in as if to confess something terrible. "You should see Levi and Jude and me at dinner time. If we're not running home to mooch off our parents, we're nuking crap food in the microwave or ordering pizza like a bunch of frat boys." She blew out a sigh and that loose curl went flying. "I need to get my own place. I need to learn a few more life skills, too. God, I need to just grow up. How sad is it that I have to crash with my younger brothers? I'm almost thirty and I sleep on their couch, Liam. *Ugh.*"

"It's not sad at all. Look, you just got back to town. As you said before, you need time to settle in, to find your footing here again. Don't forget your accomplishments— your travel blog, your photography. You touched a lot of people with your stories, Holly. Including me."

Her head tilted as she offered me a soft smile. "You're kind. Thank you for saying that." Back on Valentine's Day, I told her I had followed her online. I read her blog, followed her on Instagram, and kept up with her submissions to the various magazines and websites that published her work as best I could. She'd brushed past my admission, thanking me, but not letting the conversation get deep enough to allow me to express what her work had meant to me. She was talented but I had the feeling she didn't realize how much.

"I didn't say that just to be kind. In fact, I should thank you for the homeopathic stuff you used to share. Sadly, those posts came in handy way too often." I held my arm out to show her the burn scar running up the back. "Exhibit A."

She took my arm, turning it side to side. "Oh man, that must have hurt."

"It would have been worse, but I used that mixture with—" She ran her fingertips over my scar, and I shivered. Like I'd been sucker punched, the sudden need for more of her touch roared in my ears and I lost my words as I imagined her hand on my arm in an entirely different scenario. *Gripping, clutching, nails digging in as I—.*

"The calendula one?"

Hastily, I nodded and drew my arm back. "Yes, that's the one."

Her nose scrunched up as she watched me. Why did she have to be so cute? As if being stunningly gorgeous wasn't enough, she also had to be adorable.

"You look flushed," she told me.

I inhaled a sharp breath as the back of her hand went to my forehead before drifting down to my cheek. "I'm fine."

"Maybe you're coming down with something."

I shook my head and kept my mouth shut because nothing appropriate would come out when *you, me,* and *right now* were the only words running through my mind.

This was impossible. I'd had my hands on her body and my mouth on her lips, her neck, and that sweet little spot behind her ear that might become one of my favorites if given another chance to explore her. I'd come so close to getting everything I wanted, but I couldn't have it.

Yet.

Knock it off.

She wasn't ready for more and I was going to respect that. It was the right thing to do.

"I'll be okay. Maybe I'll go to bed early tonight," I finally answered. "I'm probably just tired." *Tired*—the universal excuse for everything. I stifled a chuckle at my own expense.

I used to imagine what it would be like to be near her, to talk to her, to touch her. And now I knew. Half of me wished I'd never found out, while the other half yearned to discover even more.

Chapter 2
Holly

"I'm home. Jude? Levi?" The door had been unlocked when I came in and the silence that greeted me was beginning to freak me out. There was probably a murderer in here waiting to chop me up. I turned on my heel and darted back to the front door.

"It's Gram! I'm in the kitchen. The boys ran to the store for me."

Jude and Levi, my younger twin brothers, rented this townhouse in one of the downtown Sweetbriar neighborhoods. I was lucky they'd decided having one of their older sisters around wouldn't cramp their style otherwise I'd still be staying with my parents. I adored my mother, but she was nosy, full of advice I didn't want to take, and constantly trying to fix me up with her friend's sons, so now I was crashing on their couch while I saved up for my own place.

Sighing with relief, I tossed my purse and coat on the coffee table and headed to the kitchen.

"Hey," I greeted. "Ooh, you're cooking. God bless you, Gram." I hugged her and kissed the top of her white curls. She was tiny; I towered over her at five-nine.

"Grab an apron, honey, and I'll teach you how to make my veggie beef soup. Levi thinks he's coming down with a cold. But I think he just wanted something home cooked. They're out picking up bread and crackers to go with the soup and a bottle of white zin for me. If I'm cooking, I'm drinking. Ain't no other way."

I laughed. "You're probably right about that. Levi is always grumbling about wanting Mom's meatloaf and trying to get me to make it."

"Like he can't learn to make it himself," she scoffed.

"That's what I'm saying!"

"He's always been a little knucklehead. But listen." She caught my eye and the serious look in hers sent a shiver up my spine.

"Oh my god, Gram. What's wrong?"

"I'm not here to make soup for the boys. I'm here for you. I have to talk to you. Sit down."

I plopped hard onto a barstool. Where were those little turds with the white zin? I knew I was going to need a drink after this; I could feel it in the air. "Tell me you don't have cancer. Is it mom? Auntie Delphine? What's happening?"

"Slow your roll, Holly," she muttered as she diced an onion. "It's nothing bad, I swear. Take a chill pill while I gather my thoughts. I have a proposition for you."

"Okay . . ." Gram was fond of shock value and the

improper use of outdated slang. Therefore, I had no idea where she was headed with this conversation.

"You remember how Grandpa and I ran that bed and breakfast before he passed?"

"Yeah . . ." After retiring from their respective careers —Gram as a nurse and Grandpa as an attorney—they opened a small bed and breakfast in town. It was in an old Victorian house near the railroad tracks. When Grandpa died about ten years ago, Gram had shut the place down and fully retired.

"Well, I'm bored. Retirement is getting old, all my soap operas have been cancelled, and I'm sick of being stuck at home. I want to open it back up."

"That's great! I used to love hanging out there." It was a stately old home with a big backyard. As a kid, I had loved to run through the gardens. Gram's thumb was as green as mine. She'd had things like a huge herb garden, roses growing on trellises, and tons of different wild-flowers to attract butterflies and hummingbirds. You name it and she had grown it.

"Good. I was hoping you'd say that. I want to open an apothecary store just like on my favorite program. I wanted to call it Rose Apothecary, but my attorney said it was too close to the show and apparently, I could be sued for that." She rolled her eyes. "So, I'll name it Rosemary Apothecary after my given name. Boring, but I'll live. You know they named the street after me, right? Rosemary Street, after the Rosemary Inn. Isn't that the cutest thing you've ever heard?" She sighed, caught up in her memories.

"I remember you telling me about that when I was little." I smiled. "And I love it! What a great idea. Good for you, Gram."

"I was hoping you'd say that too, because you're going to run it for me. We'll be partners. I'll be a silent partner and you'll be the boss. We'll split everything eighty-twenty in your favor until my investment is earned out. And we'll sell all the wonderful things you make. The oils and lotions, the sweet little soaps and cute sachets of lavender and whatever else you put in them. Oh! And the tea blends. All of it is wonderful and amazing and people are going to go nuts for it—"

My head whipped to hers, my jaw dropped, and I gaped at her for a minute before finally finding the words to speak. "Wait. Stop. Hold on a second. I can't. I don't have the skill set for such a thing. I was basically a fancy drifter for the last few years, and I still don't know what I want to do with my life. I just can't. Gram, you should ask someone else. Someone responsible and probably with a college degree or something useful to offer you—"

"Stop it," she bit out. "Don't you dare talk about my wonderful granddaughter like that." I couldn't help it— my eyes filled with tears. "I have lived vicariously through your travels, honey. You're a talented photographer and a witty writer. You have natural gift for so many things, not to mention a sparkling and hilarious personality I would like to exploit. And who is running Violet's shop right now so she can take it easy for her pregnancy? Hmm?"

"Well, none of that will pay the bills in this town,

unfortunately. And I'm only part-time at the shop. Everyone knows Vi is still in charge."

She reached for a bottle sitting on the back of the sink and brandished it at me like a weapon. "Listen here, missy. Who made this soap?"

I looked away.

"And who gave me the tea that helps me sleep every night?" I bit my lip and scrunched my eyes shut. "That she blended herself, I might add. Not to mention the lip balms and lotions and that gorgeous perfume I have on my vanity at home. And the hand-knitted blanket on my bed and my aromatherapy pillow. I could go on, but you get the picture now, don't you?"

"Uh . . ."

"Look at me, sugar pie." I looked. We didn't tell our Gram no. She was the walking, talking personification of *though she be but little she is fierce.*

"You have skills. You are a smart woman. You traveled the world, and you learned a lot of its secrets, didn't you? I am going to put you in business. You can move into the top two floors of the house. It's a done deal. I don't want any lip out of you, little miss."

"What do you mean a done deal? What have you done, Gram?"

"I hired Luke to fix the place up. He'll make any needed repairs and renovate the ground floor so we can turn it into a store. He's giving us the family discount." My brother-in-law, Luke, owned a construction company. McCabe Construction was the biggest one in the area. His father passed away while he was in the Army, and he'd taken over after his return to Sweetbriar. "Anyhoo, work will start as soon as Luke gets it on his schedule. Better get ready," she informed me with a light shrug.

"What?" I breathed. "This is too much. I think I need to lie down for a second." I stood and headed for the couch. The fetal position sounded good, and I pulled a throw blanket over my face for good measure as I curled into a ball. "I can't do this, Gram," I mumbled through the fabric as I counted backward from ten, then twenty, then thirty, to try to get a handle on my racing thoughts.

"Stop being silly and get back in here. We have soup to finish and plans to make. We'll meet with Luke soon to go over everything. We'll go out to lunch and sign papers after they're drawn up."

"Papers?"

"Yep. Luke will handle everything for us, things like building and business permits and what have you. All we have to do is tell him what we want, and he'll take care of it with his company." She waved a hand in the air. "But here's the fun part—I'm giving you half ownership of the building and leaving my share to you after I die. With a few stipulations, of course. But those won't be necessary."

"Stipulations?"

"Yeah, like I can revoke your ownership if you start running wild, or take up a drug habit, or join a cult, or something else wacky. I can't leave part of my legacy to a nutjob, of course, so don't go getting weird on me," she muttered as she puttered around the kitchen, stirring the beef browning in the pot, then adding the onions.

"Oh, okay. Yeah, well, that makes sense."

"But you're not that kind of person so it will be fine. My attorney is just a smidge overprotective."

I joined her back in the kitchen. "This might be a good idea," I conceded as I slowly warmed up to her plans. "Not the stipulations—I'm good, I promise. But the shop."

"Might? My ass. It's brilliant."

"Okay, it's probably brilliant. Can I replant the herb garden in the back?"

"Of course you can, honey. There's still rosemary and lavender running wild back there. We'll just weed-whack it a little bit, then you can do anything you need."

"Can I grow the tea myself? I've always wanted to try that. Can we have tables and chairs and a little tea corner too? With cookies and scones and tiny sandwiches?"

Her smile was smug as she answered. "Yes, we can."

"Can I do tarot card readings and crystal meditation classes?"

"Uh, sure. I don't see why not . . ."

"And I've always wanted to start an anti-hustle club—"

"What? Hustling? Remember those stipulations?" Her eyebrows rose. "No criminal activities. Remember what I said? Don't get weird on me."

I laughed. "No, Gram, one of my friends in London had one in her coffee shop. Like, everyone is always rushing around, with work, kids, smashing goals, trying to get to the top of whatever. So, she started a club for the sole purpose of relaxing. We'd knit, crochet, or sometimes paint and draw, drink tea, meditate, or just talk about books or TV shows we liked. One lady would show up every week and take a nap in a chair in the corner. The point was to just *be*. Be still, be in the moment, be present. You know?"

"I do know a little something about that. I gotcha, and I love the concept."

"Okay!" My mind ran wild with more ideas. I stood up to pace around the table.

The sound of Gram's knife on the cutting board and the sizzle of the beef in the pot for the soup kept me grounded as my mind flew with possibilities.

Could I really do this?

I ruminated on all my ideas and all the details and all the effort it would take to get it up and running and, crashing back to earth, I sank into a chair. "I don't know if I can do this."

"No negativity," she tutted. "The only thing holding you back right now, honey, is you. Now that doesn't mean the playing field will ever be level or that there won't be real obstacles to get in our way. But it's your life and it's up to you to make it what you want it to be. You said you're ready to be home, to plant roots and make a place for yourself here. Didn't you?"

"Yeah, I do want that, so much." I was through with long-term travel. Any sense of wanderlust I had left in my heart had burned itself out once I started spending time with my family again and started getting to know my nieces and nephews better.

"I want it too. I missed my little Hollyberry. And I want you to be happy you're staying in town. This feels right to me, sugar pie, and I think we can do something great together. Don't forget how much you loved it when Grandpa and I ran the inn. You'd help me in the garden and, well, you didn't help me bake, but you did assist in disposing of the broken cookies, didn't you?" She shot me a wink.

"Yes, I remember, and I agree. This feels like it could be perfect for me. Almost too good to be true . . ."

"And I might add, there's plenty of bedrooms on the top two floors of the house if you, perhaps, find yourself a fella and want to give me some more great-grandbabies. Like with that cutie patootie, Liam, maybe?"

Cutie Patootie? Liam was more like a five-alarm smokeshow. But that was not the point right now. My family's penchant for matchmaking was the real problem.

"Not you too, Gram. Please? I get enough of that from Mom."

"I'm just saying, he's a sweet boy. Easy on the eyes too. I go to his house from time to time with a batch of my snickerdoodles to watch *Schitt's Creek* on his big TV with him. But whatever you say, I'll stay out of it. Your Gram will be your safe place. For rants, complaints, or hiding out from the gentlemen suitors your mom is determined to send in your direction."

"It's appreciated. You have no idea how much."

The door crashed open as my brothers entered. "We're back!"

"No more talk about gentleman suitors please," I hissed in alarm. "Jude has a terrible habit of blabbing everything he hears to Mom. It's his toxic trait. Give him some banana bread and a glass of chocolate milk and he becomes an open book. *Shh.*"

"Oh yeah, I know all about that. How do you think I knew you wanted to stay in town this time? You didn't tell me anything about your plans yourself, missy. And for future reference, carrot cake also gets his lips a-flappin'. Oh, he also knows about the Liam situation too, so heads up."

My cheeks heated. Did anyone *not* know about my little—okay, massive—crush? "Sorry about that. I should have told you I was staying in Sweetbriar myself. And we're not talking about Liam today, okay? Maybe not ever."

She waved her knife in the air. "You're forgiven. We have bigger fish to fry together now."

Jude burst into the kitchen and placed the grocery bag on the counter, unearthing a loaf of crusty bread and a bottle of wine. "That smells so good."

"Of course it does. Your grandma doesn't mess around when her babies are sick." She shot me another wink and I shook my head.

He twisted the corkscrew into the wine bottle with a laugh. "Right. About that. Levi's on the couch keeping up the act." He kissed Gram's cheek. "Thanks for coming over."

"Of course. Set the table, honey. We'll eat in a couple hours. Once the pot gets going, you're going to have to keep it stirred. Holly and I have things to discuss."

"No problem." He raised his eyebrows at me over top of Gram's head.

She directed Jude to the cutting board. "Dump these veggies into the pot, add the stock, then give it a stir. Holly, come on, we're going out to the patio to brainstorm. Grab that notebook off the table. We'll make a list of all the supplies you'll need so when the shop opens, we'll be ready to go. Your mama said we can store everything in their garage." She swiped two glasses from the cupboard and the bottle of wine and gestured for me to follow her outside.

It seemed we were about to plan the rest of my life. I trailed behind her with a smile on my face and for the first time in years, I felt like I might be more than what I ever thought I could be.

Chapter 3
Liam

After our conversation, I'd stayed away from Violet's shop. Being around Holly was just too much for me. The temptation to push for more than what she wanted was nearly overwhelming. I never should have kissed her; now I knew what I was missing. It could be so good between us.

Just friends . . .

I focused on the drive home to get her out of my mind. I marveled at how far I had come from my Ranger days. Desert to forest. It was like a living landscape painting up here. Once I turned off the highway, the road narrowed, turning serpentine as I drove straight into the Mt. Hood National Forest. When the weather was bad, the drive was as treacherous as it was beautiful.

After his father passed away, Luke had inherited about thirty or so acres of this gorgeous Oregon land, a few million dollars, and the family construction business that he'd hired me to work for after we left the Army.

Both of us had been medically discharged after an attack our unit had suffered. He lived here with his childhood sweetheart, Lily, who was now his wife, and their kids. When I'd first arrived I rented a house in town, but had since taken over his original family home—a modest log cabin tucked into the trees at the back of this extensive property—while he and his family moved into the newer house up near the road.

If I didn't know where to go, I'd never find the place. The sign for his private street was buried within the trees that lined the road so closely I could reach out my window and touch them if I wanted to. Sometimes, I did.

Ivy and moss wreathed the tall pines, while gnarled roots embedded the earth and twisted branches rose to the sky like timeless examples of how to hold on. How to keep steady in the midst of a world that seemed determined to knock everything down.

I lowered my windows, immersing myself in the dusky, verdant beauty surrounding me. Early spring in Sweetbriar was often still tinged by winter cold and today was no exception. There was a bite in the air. I shivered as I turned onto the long winding driveway that led to Luke's place.

Cutting the engine, I stared at the huge log cabin-slash-mansion my friend Luke now lived in as I exited my truck. The full force of how different my life had become hit me as I felt the cool mountain mist against my skin and took in all the green that surrounded me. The last ten years faded further and further away the more time I spent here, like sand blowing by in the breeze, but it still weighed on my soul—and probably always would.

"Uncle Liam's here!"

Luke's six-year-old son, Dylan, ran to me from the wrap-around front porch. I picked him up and swung him in a circle. "Hey, little man."

"Higher!" I chuckled and lifted him over my head. "You're the tallest ever!" Peals of laughter washed over me as I sat him down. Damn, I loved this kid. "Tomorrow is puppy day at Papa Jed's so I finally get to hold them! Are you going to go see them too?"

"I just came from there." Luke's grandfather was a Vietnam vet who trained service dogs on his ranch. He also ran a support group that I attended along with Luke and a few other vets who lived in the area.

"Were they cute? Did you get to hold them?"

"They are and nope, because tomorrow is the official day. Jed said you would be the first."

"I can't wait!" He took off running into the house as Luke was coming out.

"Hey. Have you heard about the puppies?" He grinned at me as he approached.

"A few times." I chuckled.

"He's talked about nothing else since they were born. Don't be surprised if Rocky gets a puppy buddy to hang with." Rocky was a brown and white boxer Luke had gotten from Jed's ranch, and had done a lot for Luke's state of mind.

I turned at the sound of a car pulling in behind me, smiling when I spotted Holly and Rose, Lily's identical twin, pulling up behind my truck. Her cheeks flushed pink, and she waved when she saw me. I had never seen a woman as beautiful as her. Each time I saw her I lost my breath.

"What are they doing here tonight? Are you having a party?"

"Sister shit," he answered. "Ice cream and movies. Vi will be here too, if she's feeling better—morning sickness has been kicking her butt lately."

"I wanted to go wine tasting down at Briarwood Falls but half of us are preggers." Rose let out a heavy sigh as she approached us while Holly laughed. "Today was an entire day. I'm exhausted, but I have taken a sacred vow never to miss sister time now that all of us are finally in town together again."

"I could definitely go for a glass too." Holly agreed. "Fridays at the shop are insane. Remember that weird rush last time you were there, Liam? It was like that today too."

I simply nodded in response. My heart raced; I was too surprised to see her to answer with words. I felt like a kid again, stuck back in high school with a stupid crush. By now I should be used to the way my body reacted to having her near me. But each time I caught sight of her still had me reeling, sending my heartbeat out of control and my mind into overdrive trying to fight her pull.

"I have wine," Luke offered. "And I'm smoking a rack of ribs out back. I know it's late, but Lily had a craving."

"Ice cream and ribs sounds great." The sound of

Holly's throaty laughter stole what was left of my thoughts as I watched a smile unfurl across her face.

"Don't forget about the wine," Rose said. "Do you need any help?"

"Nope, I got it. Lily is in the living room. Go relax and I'll bring you both a glass."

"You're the best, Lukey." Rose reached high and pinched his cheeks. "Later, guys."

"Later . . ." My eyes trailed after Holly, an idiotic smile spreading across my face as I watched her walk up the porch steps.

"Listen, before we go inside, I have news. I have a job for you."

"What? Huh?" In a daze, I slowly shifted my eyes to Luke. Why did that sound so ominous? Like a test or a call to action. My face blanked in confusion. Still distracted by Holly, it took me a beat before continuing. "What's the job?"

"You seem a little out of it." He studied my face. "Have you been getting enough sleep?"

"Not really." Since returning home, I suffered frequent bouts of insomnia. It was getting better but was still a pain in the ass.

"Want to talk about it?" We had started making it a point to share whenever we felt out of sorts. Both of us were determined not to succumb to our PTSD ever again. Therapy, support, and communication were what would continue to pull us through and keep us healthy.

"Nah, don't worry. It's nothing we haven't covered before. I'm just feeling a bit restless lately is all." *Yeah, because I'm falling for your sister-in-law, who you grew up with and love like she was your own little sister.* I shook my head to clear it.

"I get you. Maybe you should start dating again? Or find a like-minded woman, and, you know—"

"Uh-uh, not ready for that." I was not about to start dating someone when my feelings for Holly were so strong. No matter how long it had been, it wouldn't be right to lead someone on.

He held out his hands with a grin. "Fair enough. I'm not here to push you into anything. It was just a suggestion."

"No worries. I get you. So, what's the job?"

"Holly is going into business. She's going to start up an apothecary store in Rosemary's old bed and breakfast in town. You're going to oversee the renovation. Owen will get it started with demo, clean up, and giving the outside a fresh coat of paint. Then you'll step in for the rest of the project. I know you want out of the office and into some builds and remodels. This will be the perfect place to get that going."

"Wait a minute. Owen? Are you sure about that? I still can't believe you hired him." He was a good worker and Luke had known him since childhood. But at one point he'd been engaged to Holly. From what I'd heard, she broke things off a day before their wedding after she found out he had cheated on her. He had a terrible reputation around town as a philanderer. As far as I was concerned, Owen was on thin ice, and I'd be keeping a close eye on him.

"He'll be fine. I asked Holly if she was okay with it, and she said it was ancient history and she didn't care. She won't be there while he does demo work anyway. I don't want to fire him, I'd feel terrible. He has five kids, Liam. Plus, we grew up together—"

"I still think you give too many chances. Plus, this could potentially end up being a huge issue. But, yeah, I mean, get where you're coming from, I guess." I paused. "Okay, no, I don't get it. He's bad for business. I'm still pretty new in town and even I have heard about how much he cheats on his wife." I was still getting used to living in a small town. Everyone in Sweetbriar either grew up together, used to be neighbors, or ran into each other regularly at Violet's for coffee or the Quickbriar Stop and Go for gas. The main point being everyone knew everyone's business, cut each other far too much slack for my liking, and put up with too much of each other's bullshit. I was way too suspicious to fight what had always been my first instinct, which was to doubt everyone and everything.

"That's why you're in charge of this project. He'll never be lead, and I won't assign him to any job where he will be in a situation to even speak to anyone. He'll work on empty properties or with a crew. Don't worry about that. I just don't want his wife and kids to lose their house and starve. I'd do it myself, but I'm already spread too thin with other projects as it is. Plus, I know I can trust you to get this exactly right."

I threw a hand up and stopped him. "No need to

explain. It's fine. I don't want his kids to starve either. I'll do it."

What was I getting myself into? Now I'd have to see her at work, rather than just my brief visits to Violet's and occasional run-ins here at Luke's place, both of which were easy to nip in the bud by using work as an excuse to rush off. *Or not.* I'd had coffee with her earlier. *What had I been thinking?* Fuck, this was a bad idea.

"Thank you. The file is on your desk at the office. Rosemary is chomping at the bit to get this done."

I couldn't stop myself from asking. "And Holly?" I'd heard nothing about this project and it felt like he'd known about it for a while, which was odd. We always discussed everything to do with the business.

"I was sworn to secrecy. Rosemary wanted to have everything lined up and ready to go before she said anything to Holly. She didn't want to risk disappointing her if it ended up being too expensive or if the place was too run down to make it work."

"That makes sense. How's the building?"

"It's been empty for over a decade, but it's solid. It won't take much to get it up and running. Should be a quick turnaround. Three months, tops. Maybe a little longer if we have supply delays. You know how that goes."

Three months.

I could handle three months. I'd handled a lot worse in my life. What could be so hard about seeing one beautiful, irresistible woman day in and day out compared to what I'd done in the Army?

"Great. Perfect. I'm going to head home and try to get some sleep."

"I thought we were going to talk. And what about the ribs?" His eyes narrowed on mine. He knew something was off with me, but Holly was the one thing I couldn't discuss with him. Not yet anyway, and maybe not ever. "You're always invited, you know that right? No matter who is here. You're family, Liam."

"I know, and it's appreciated. I'm just tired."

"Okay." His shoulders relaxed as the tension left. He believed me. "Take it easy. Get some rest and I'll see you tomorrow."

Tired. That excuse worked every time. I headed to my truck to go to my place and hopefully get some damn rest.

Chapter 4
Liam

I awoke gasping for air, covered in a cold sweat, and shivering in the dark of my bedroom. Shadows shifting and swirling across my ceiling had become an all-too-familiar sight and I was sick of it. I flipped to my stomach and punched my pillow with a growl. I was frustrated, fucking tired beyond belief, and not sure what to do about it beyond what I'd been doing. Therapy, my support group, and talking things out with Luke had worked for everything else, but not my insomnia.

As soon as I got home from Luke's I'd showered and went to bed, falling asleep almost the second my body hit the mattress. But it didn't last. Maybe I required complete exhaustion. Or maybe there was something I was missing. Therapy could only do so much; how could I talk about the shit buried in my subconscious when I didn't even fucking remember it?

I threw my legs over the side of the mattress, scooting it back into place as I stood. With a flick, I turned my bedside light on, squinting against the sudden glare. After a quick glance I located my shorts, grabbed my socks, shoes, and keys, and headed out the front door to wear myself out.

The bite of the cold air felt good on my bare skin as I took off on a slow jog, gaining speed the closer I got to the road.

I never used to have trouble with sleep. I used to be able to crash anywhere—on the ground, in a truck, surrounded by dust and heat, with my senses filled with unbearable sounds and smells. But easy sleep ended after my discharge.

I knew I had left part of myself behind when I left the hospital. All I could recall was waking up in a truck bed with my head in Luke's lap and him telling me to hold on as he tried to staunch the endless flow of blood coming from my back and head. He'd saved my life but was unable to save the rest of our unit. Our positions in the front of the Humvee had spared our lives. I was grateful I hadn't let him drive, or he would have almost died instead of me. He had a family who needed him. What did I have? I had nothing. *Not yet, anyway.*

The wounds to my back had been primarily superficial. The few deeper ones had been stitched up and had since healed. The head injury had been more serious. I'd been knocked unconscious and left with a concussion. It had wiped my memory clean and left me with recurring headaches. My back and scalp were now riddled with scars left by the shrapnel from the IED explosion that had taken our unit out and because I was the driver, I'd developed a sense of guilt that I had not been able to shake off.

Between therapy and Luke telling me what had gone down, I knew there was nothing I could have done to prevent the attack, but the guilt still lingered. It came in fleeting waves—illusory, enigmatic, and baffling, because while rationally I knew I held no blame for what had happened, that logic held no power over my subconscious mind and my feelings often came at me the hardest when I was asleep. I knew I had nightmares; the state of my bed upon waking had made that fact all too clear.

And then there was the one thing I didn't want to remember at all and still can't believe I'd done. A few months back—the day my grandmother died—I got black-out drunk and came to my senses with a gun in my hand. Luke and Lily had broken down my door, their terrified eyes the first thing to register in my brain as Luke's dog, Rocky, inserted himself between the gun and my head. Luke took it from me, disassembled it, and when I returned home, he helped me get rid of it.

The alarm and worry on their faces were something I never wanted to see again. It was the reason why I refused to take medication to sleep or get drunk ever again. I needed to be in my right mind, always.

I remembered feeling alone that day.

I remembered no longer being able to handle the unbearable crushing weight of solitude. I had wanted to feel something else, anything but the relentless fucking tragedy my life seemed to always be drowning in.

But I couldn't remember actually wanting to die.

I don't want to die.

Even though I was the last one left in my family, deep down I knew I still had a lot to live for and I wanted to make them proud. I couldn't reconcile what I had done with how I felt now that I had been getting help. The feelings wouldn't sort into something I could explain, even to myself. Maybe I would always wonder what had gotten into me that day.

My grandmother had raised me after my parents died and I had no siblings. My dad passed from lung cancer when I was ten, then my mother was killed four years later by a drunk driver while on her way to pick me up from school. Luke's mother had passed the same way; it was one of the things that had bonded us. He was like a brother to me and I didn't want to let him down. After what we'd been through, we needed each other. Somehow, no matter how messed up we got over the years, we had managed to keep each other steady. Until that one day.

My grandmother would have been so disappointed in me; she'd be horrified that I chose to get wasted the day she died instead of honoring her memory by doing something useful. Maybe that's what's been keeping me up at night—not being able to make it right with her. She had taught me the importance of forgiveness, of being understood, and never letting the sun set on your bad feelings. God, how I wished I could talk to her one last time.

Enough.

I'd come outside to ease my mind, to clear it. Not get

bogged down and buried in nostalgia and loss and grief over things I had no power to change.

I ran a hand over my beard as I reached the gate at the front of Luke's property. I would jog into town, go to the office, take a nap, then get an early start on the day. There was a shower in the office suite I shared with Luke. I kept spare clothes and essentials there and I could always catch a ride home tonight with Luke or Lily.

Letting the sound of my footsteps on the pavement calm me, I kept my breath steady as I upped my pace and sprinted. Running down hill was always a rush. Street-lamps shone below as I ran along the bluff overlooking town, but I saw no headlights. Sweetbriar was still asleep. *Like I should be.*

Rounding a curve, I once again had the forest at my side. The air cooled as my sneakers crunched over the dried pine needles dusting the road. Rustling sounds in the distance caught my ear and I slowed, something moving fast through the brush set me on alert. I didn't stop, but I kept my eyes trained on the edge of the forest as I ran. Moonlight shot spikes through the trees, but it wasn't enough light to discern what was headed my way. The sounds, both muted and sharp at the same time, confused me. It was unlike any animal I'd ever heard out here. The creature seemed to run with purpose. I'd only observed animals running like that if they were chasing something, or if they were the one being chased. The pace was steady until who or whatever it was fell.

"Fucking damn it!" I stopped short at the gasping voice in the distance.

Squinting against the dark, I darted into a shadow to conceal my presence. Hands to my knees, I tried to slow my breath as I stepped off the road and watched a shadowy figure staggering toward me in the distance. The shards of moonlight through the trees only illuminated them enough for me to know it was a person, not an animal. My heart rate was up, I was breathing hard, and it was loud. Bark scratched my bare back as I tried to blend into my surroundings.

"*Ugh*, dang mud! Ouch, damn it." The voice was female, breathless, and tremulous. She was scared.

"Do you need help?" I called out.

"No," was the answering shriek. "Stay away from me." Her pace quickened as she drew closer to me and not farther away as I suspected was her intention.

"I'm not here to hurt anyone. I was just out for a run —" I stepped into a small clearing in the trees just as she burst through the other side and crashed into me, knocking us both to the forest floor.

Dried brush and dead bark scratched my back, and I lost my breath as her body landed on mine.

"Leave me alone!" Her hands scrambled for purchase on my chest as she tried to get up.

"Let me help you. Are you hurt?" My words didn't seem to register as she rolled to the side and stood.

"I need to get to my sister's house—" A thread of hysteria tinged her voice and at that moment I realized who she was.

"Holly?"

She froze, watching me carefully as I stood. "Liam.

Oh thank god, it's you." Her voice broke and she inhaled a shaky breath.

"Yeah, it's me. What's going on?"

"I was out for a jog. I couldn't sleep. I was almost to the high school track—it's where I always used to go . . ." She scrubbed a hand beneath her eyes, clearly crying. I wanted to hold her. I wanted to get her safe. Then I wanted to hunt down who or whatever had scared her and get them gone. "Anyway, I got the strangest feeling someone was watching me. It spooked me so I decided to cut through the forest and head for Lily's house instead. It's closer than going back home and I know I'm almost there, but like an idiot, I got scared. I panicked and I fell and . . . I-I had an . . . accident before I came back to Sweetbriar. I think maybe I just relived it a little bit."

An accident?

I wanted to know what had happened to her, but now was clearly not the time to ask. Even in the dark I could tell her cheeks were red. She was embarrassed to be caught afraid like this.

Her shoulders shook with a sob, and I could take no more. I held out my arms, gratified when she closed the distance between us and threw herself against me. "Shh," I soothed, wrapping her tight as I scanned the dark over her shoulder.

It was quiet.

The noises I had heard had most likely come from her.

"Thank god you were out here," she mumbled as she tucked her cheek into my chest.

I used one hand to rub gentle circles in the center of her back as I stared into the woods, scanning for anything unusual. I registered the feel of her against the skin of my bare chest but knew now was not the time to focus on that. Holly was terrified and needed reassurance, and I would make sure she stayed safe. "I got you. I won't let anyone hurt you."

"Okay," she whispered, sagging against me in relief. "Thank you."

"But let's get out of here. Just in case someone really is following you. Yeah?"

"Lily's place is just up the road." She pulled back. "Can we go to your house? Now that you're here and I know I'm not about to be murdered, I'd feel stupid waking her up. I probably lost my shit over nothing."

"Absolutely."

"Why are you out right now? Three in the morning is both too early and too late for this to be part of your regular routine." After pulling out of our hug, she had relaxed a bit. I had not.

"You're right, it's not my usual time. I couldn't sleep either." I was waiting for something to pop out and attack us. I almost wanted it to happen so I could work all the charged emotion out of my system. If someone was after her I wouldn't feel bad about it.

"Insomnia sucks."

"You got that right," I muttered as I turned to walk backward a few feet, scanning the woods behind us as we made our way back to the road.

"Do you hear anything? I don't. I probably just got

spooked by leftover horror movie vibes, or maybe I heard an animal. I don't usually freak out like this." She let out a deep sigh. "I mean, I've hiked the Pacific Crest Trail by myself. I've crashed in a lot of sketchy places over the years and staying out past my bedtime is my favorite thing to do. But, damn, tonight was weird, it reminded me of—uh, my accident." She grabbed my hand and held it tight as we continued up the hill toward my place.

"What happened?" The question was deliberately open ended. She could tell me about her accident or what had just happened.

"Have you ever felt—? This is going to sound so stupid . . ." Silence loomed between us. I got the sense she was still embarrassed as I observed the tense lines crossing her face and she avoided my eyes.

"I'm not going to push you to tell me anything. But keeping stuff inside is never good. Listen, I would never judge you for being scared. It's dark as hell out here—spooky, too. Plus, Luke won't shut up about trying to find Bigfoot. That has to be embedded in the back of your mind somewhere, right? I got the feeling it's been a long-standing obsession of his."

A laugh burst out of her. "Oh lord, yes, ever since we were all kids, he'd have us following grids all through the forest out here trying to find traces of him. I can't believe he's not over it by now. And, okay, yeah, you're totally right about keeping things inside. But let's talk about it when we get to your place. When I'm not covered in mud and freezing my ass off. When we can lock the door and look into the woods from behind a closed window, preferably with you standing next to me looking all mean and threatening."

"You got it. I can do mean and threatening." I entered the code to Luke's gate to let us onto the property, shutting it firmly behind us after we passed through.

She looked up at me with a small smile. "Don't forget sweet and protective."

"Never. Those are my top two traits. I'm also relentlessly charming. It's pretty fucking irresistible, isn't it?" I teased to lighten her mood. I couldn't stand to see her scared.

Her eyes shone bright in the pale light of the moon as she tried and failed to suppress a giggle. "You are completely and totally riddled with charm. God, Liam, how? I'm laughing in the dark when only moments ago I was terrified and about to pee my pants in a mud puddle."

"It's a gift." I shrugged lightly and returned her smile. "Come on." I offered my arm, her smile turned shy as she looped hers through mine with her hand clutching my bicep.

"I hope you have tea. Or coffee. Ooh, hot chocolate!" She bumped into my side as we walked the distance through Luke's property to my place. "I'm about to raid your fridge so hard. But I'll restock it, I promise."

"I have all of those." I grinned down at her. "And what's mine is yours. I make a mean breakfast too. Are you hungry?"

"Starved. Running through the forest like a bat out of hell took it out of me. And that doesn't even get into the emotional disarray my brain is in. I'm scattered and starving, Liam. I need to eat my feelings real bad. Thank goodness one of us can cook because all the restaurants in town are closed at this hour."

We made it to my porch and reluctantly, I let her go to unlock the door. "I got you covered. Are you in the mood for sweet or savory? Bacon and eggs or pancakes and maple syrup?"

"Would you think less of me if I said both? And what are you doing with maple syrup in your house?" She poked my abs with a laugh. Goose bumps scattered over my skin as I shivered involuntarily beneath her brief touch.

"Hey, I make banana pancakes and maple syrup is natural, okay? I hope you're not opposed to turkey bacon."

"I love it. And I'm only teasing you. You know that, right?"

"I know." My voice dropped low. "Don't ever stop."

I heard her quick intake of breath as she looked up at me through her lashes. "I don't think I can."

"Good." I'd intended to tease her, but the gruff growl in my voice betrayed me. There was so much more I wanted to say right now, but I refrained. Forcing my eyes away from her gorgeous silhouette in the dark, I opened the door and stepped aside to let her in first, praying I had enough control to keep my ever-growing feelings to myself.

Chapter 5
Holly

I passed through the front door, curious to see what he'd done with the place. I hadn't been here in years, not since I was a little kid and me and my siblings were dropped off to play with Luke. He flicked on the light, and I flinched against the glare.

How had I forgotten he was shirtless? The sight of him chased all the residual fear from my forest flashback out of my head and I was glad. I didn't want to think about it anyway.

My mouth ran dry. He was built like a dang statue; The David had nothing on him. Broad shoulders and a chiseled chest tapered down to an impressive set of carved out abs. He was perfect from head to toe and wearing a pair of cut-off gray sweatpants and sneakers. Then he turned around to lock the door and I gasped. He was covered with scars. They traversed the planes of his back in a patternless story of pain. Some were small, superficial, and already faded pink, like little ribbons. But a few were raised and still an angry red.

"Oh my god, your back."

He whipped around to face me. "I'm okay. It's healed."

"Oh, Liam . . ."

"Shit. I'm fine, really." He started to back away but stopped when I reached out.

I traced a fingertip over a thick curving scar running over his shoulder to end at the side of his neck. "This must have hurt so bad. Scar tissue can be painful even if the wound is healed. Turn around and let me see the rest. I bet I can help."

With his eyes locked to mine, he remained frozen for a moment. Then he turned, breaking contact. His head dropped. "Yeah, it gets uncomfortable sometimes—" His voice broke off midsentence; he'd shut down. I sensed his vulnerability and found myself wanting to prove I was someone he could trust. Someone he could share his pain and insecurities with, someone safe.

Was he embarrassed? The thought filled my heart with almost unbearable tenderness.

My heart ached for him while my body grew overwhelmed with sensation from his nearness. I wanted to throw myself into his arms again but had no reason to do so. "Um, I have a few remedies I could use. Massage, essential oils, various creams . . . Will you let me try to help you?"

"Yeah, sure. Actually, I would love that." His voice

was rough—husky and deep. It sent a thrill down my spine.

The deep growl of his words and the thought of having my hands all over that broad, heavily muscled back of his almost did me in. Heat flooded my veins and I slammed my eyes shut against the rising tide of naughty mental images, alarmed because the sexy thoughts were now mingled with thoughts of holding him, healing him, chasing away all the things that kept him up at night. I cleared my throat as I tried to clear my brain. "Okay, good. When I get home, I'll make a list of what I'll need, then we can make a plan. Once I get settled, I'm going start doing massage therapy again at my shop."

"I appreciate it, and anytime you're available will work for me." A smile worked its way through the uncertainty that had clouded his expression before and I returned it, thrilled that he was willing to let me help him.

"Okay," I breathed. I wanted him to be comfortable with me. I wanted to be the one to make him feel better. The question of *why* danced around in my thoughts, but I shoved it aside. He deserved this.

His body jolted suddenly, as if he had come to his senses or out of a spell. "God, Holly. Where are my manners? You're shivering. Would you like a shower while I make breakfast? You weren't kidding about being covered with mud." He brushed a clump of muddy hair over my shoulder with a teasing wink. Charming Liam was back, and I was stunned that he could flip the switch so quickly. "I'll loan you a T-shirt. In fact, I should grab one for myself too and wipe off this mud." His cheeks flushed red above his beard as he ran a hand down his chest, drawing attention to each of the glorious, rippling muscles adorning his torso.

"I'm sorry I got you dirty." I cleared my throat. *Gah! Double entendre much?* "So, a shower? Yes, please. I think I'm starting to get crusty. Like, I love a good mud bath, but stumbling into a puddle while scared out of my mind isn't my preferred method," I joked to cover my attraction to him. Flirting with him would be a bad idea.

"I bet." His grin was irresistibly devastating. He confused me; I couldn't tell if he was trying to flirt with me or if this was just his natural state and he'd found his way back into it. Or perhaps he really was insecure about his scars and covering it up with his seemingly ingrained flirtatious charm. I hadn't spent enough time with him to know for sure. I couldn't read him yet, but I wanted to.

I smiled without answering, unsure of how to respond without giving myself away. Even though I'd told him after our Valentine's Day kiss that we could only be friends, it didn't erase the attraction shimmering in the air between us.

"Come on. Let's get you cleaned up." He gestured for me to follow him down the hall. "There's a stack of clean towels in the cupboard, and I'll grab a shirt for you to put on after."

"Thank you so much, Liam. I'm so lucky you were out tonight." Good manners trumped all uncertainty, and I was glad to be back on sure footing again.

"Me too. You have no idea. Having you here is so

much better than staring at the ceiling alone unable to sleep." He left me in the bathroom as he continued down the hall to his bedroom.

I rummaged around for a towel, deciding to go with the flow. Tonight was weird and I'd chalk up any questions about his mood to that. Mine too, for that matter. "Can I help myself to your shampoo and stuff?" I called out.

"Yep." He popped his head in and tossed me a faded black T-shirt. "Here you go. I'll get the food started. Take your time."

"Oh, I intend to. I'm gonna use up all your hot water." I brandished the rolled-up T-shirt at him for emphasis. "And hey, I'm no help in the kitchen but I can do clean-up duty like a champ. So don't do any dishes. I got that part covered." Unfortunately, he was now wearing a shirt, otherwise I'd be eye-to-spectacular-pec level with him, damn it.

He reached up, grasping the frame of the doorway with a broad palm as he leaned forward with a smirk, dipping his head so we were now eye to eye. "I make no promises. My mom was a clean-as-you-go cook and that's how I learned. I'm afraid it's a habit now."

I let out an exaggerated joking gasp. "Are you the perfect man, Liam? Rescuing distressed damsels in the middle of the night then cooking them a well-balanced breakfast once you get them back to your adorable woodsy lair?"

"Far from it." He pushed back with a laugh and

stepped into the hall. "Like I said before, what's mine is yours. Use whatever you need."

"Thanks . . ." I murmured to his retreating back as I tried to calm my racing heart.

Contrary to what I'd told Liam, I hurried through my shower, chagrined to realize I didn't want to miss a moment with him tonight and a little bit freaked about how my tiny (massive) crush on him seemed to be growing bigger by the second. After tonight, I'd keep my distance. It was better for us both; I couldn't get into a relationship when my life was such a mess. No one deserved to get sucked into that.

I pulled my undies on, not thrilled to be re-wearing them, but what else could I do? If I went out there commando I'd be far too tempted to crawl into his lap and go for a ride or do something else equally dumb and probably orgasmically awesome. I slipped into his T-shirt with a low moan. It smelled like laundry soap and him, it was old and soft as silk, and it went down almost to my knees. "I'm keeping this T-shirt," I yelled into the hall as I opened the door. "What's yours is mine, remember?" I teased.

He eyed me speculatively as I rounded the corner into the kitchen. "Hmm, I'll have to think about it. I love that shirt. But you look so good wearing it, so I might just let you have it."

"Think about it all you want. I can be stealthy when I need to be. Maybe I'll just steal it."

"Stealthy? Like tonight when you were sneaking through the forest oh-so quietly?"

"Ha. Touché, Liam." I laughed and flopped into a barstool at the island counter. It smelled awesome in here. Like bacon and chocolate and everything homey and good in the world. My fears were carried away on steamy, yummy-smelling flavor clouds as I watched him move competently around his kitchen.

"I'm sorry. That was mean and probably too soon to joke about. Here, try this." He slid a mug across the counter then carefully ladled in some hot chocolate from a steaming saucepan. "Let me make it up to you. As you requested, hot chocolate. Made from scratch, not a packet."

"Ooooh. Aren't you fancy." He watched me avidly, lips quirked expectantly at the corner as I blew across the top of the steaming mug then took a sip. My eyebrows shot up. "It tastes like hot melted ice cream. Oh my god." Screw my messed-up life. I should marry him right now and let him cook for me the rest of my life, preferably shirtless. Then later I could pantslessly thank him after I cleaned up his kitchen.

He chuckled at my food moans as I sipped the hot chocolate. "Breakfast is almost ready. We can eat at the coffee table."

"That sounds perfect." *Because pre-dawn breakfasts on a cozy sofa with the crush you can't have were such a smart thing to do.*

I had to change the subject, take us back to somewhere inane, meaningless, *friendly*. "So, did my mother invite you to Sunday dinner? I missed the last couple. She's probably mad at me."

That ought to kill the mood. My mother and I hadn't been getting along lately. When you come from a family full of perfect people it could be hard to fit in. Eventually I quit trying and did my own thing. But she was still determined to fix my life and fix me up and since I was determined to *not* be fixed, we now had a problem.

Valentine's Day had been the last straw. I'd hid in the coffee shop's back room with Liam while she tried to get me to dance/talk/date Jared Jamison. I can't believe he snatched my cell phone like he did, the dumb jerk. He'd had a crush on me since we were kids, but I just didn't like him that way and never would. He had always been persistent but had never gone too far. Now that I was single and back in town, his determination to go out with me had ramped back up and I was getting fed up with the entire situation.

"She did. Are you going?"

"Doubtful. She won't stop trying to fix me up."

His expression soured. "Like with that asshole from Violet's who snatched your phone?"

"Yep, his name is Jared and we've known each other since we were kids. My mother has been friends with his mom forever. She's an awesome lady but her son is a pest. Let's just say he got lucky. If it had been anyone else, I would have taught him a lesson on what the word *no* means."

"I'll teach him a lesson for you," he muttered. "Just say the word."

"Oh, don't worry. Ultimately, he's harmless. He

caught me off guard, but it won't happen again. I'm onto him now."

A grunt was his only response as he turned off the stove and plated our food.

"Can I help?"

"Yeah, grab our mugs and some napkins and follow me."

I followed him to the living room, watching the muscles in his back move as he walked. He'd put a shirt on, but it didn't hide a single sexy ripple. I sat our mugs down then sat my booty down, suddenly becoming acutely aware that I was dressed only in undies and a T-shirt—*his* T-shirt.

It was not that I didn't trust Liam. I did. Luke and my family wouldn't love him so much if he were a creeper. I didn't trust myself. I had things to work out before I could be with anyone, but I found myself wanting to be with him far too much for my own good.

"This looks great." I took a bite of banana pancake and barely bit back the groan threatening to escape. "Delicious. You have to give me the recipe so I can screw it up."

"It's pretty easy. One banana, two eggs. That's it."

"I think it might be the flipping I have a problem with. I think I flip too early and end up making a mess."

"I'll teach you. You fix my back and maybe I can teach you to cook." His voice was sleepy. I watched fascinated while his chest expanded and contracted as a huge yawn escaped him.

"Tired?" I said through my own yawn. I guess they really were contagious.

He rolled his shoulders then stretched his arms over his head. "I slept about an hour, but it feels like I've been up for days."

"Yeah, Jude and Levi are both on overnight shifts at the firehouse all week and I guess I don't like being alone anymore. I don't know . . ."

He leaned toward me, and his voice lowered. "You decided to go for a run to exhaust yourself, didn't you?"

I tilted my head and nodded.

"I did the same thing," he confessed.

"And now here we are." My voice came out shakier than I liked as I recalled my crazed sprint through the forest.

"What happened out there tonight, Holly?" He asked quietly, eyes alight with sympathy.

I met his gaze with a sideways glance. "I think I was on the verge of a panic attack. I don't think anything actually happened tonight. I never used to be scared of anything, but lately everything scares me. The dark, being alone . . . you name it and it freaks me out. You even freak me out, Liam."

His head whipped back. "Me? Why?"

"Somehow you're getting me to admit things to you that I won't even admit to myself."

"Well, you do the same thing. To me."

"Oh yeah?"

He nodded.

"I guess we really are friends then."

When he spoke again, his voice was tender. "Seems like it."

"Good. I mean, who doesn't need more friends, right?"

He reached out and patted my hand. My body went electric at his brief touch, and I think his did too because he drew his hand back like I'd shocked him.

We finished our breakfast in silence, but it wasn't awkward. At this point, we were each way too tired to feel any sort of embarrassment. It felt like we'd been through something with each other tonight. Like we'd bonded. Like we were real friends now—friends with possibilities, I decided. I just needed to get my shit together.

Chapter 6
Liam

I woke up sprawled on my couch with sunlight in my eyes and a sleeping Holly draped across my chest. I had one leg on the floor while the other was bent and resting high between hers. The soft warm heat of her center was pressed tight to the bare skin of my thigh with only her panties between us.

At some point in the night we had fallen asleep, but how we had ended up like this, I did not know. We were intertwined, her cheek rested near my collarbone with one arm thrown around my waist to hang off the couch, and the other on my neck. My hands were full of her gorgeous ass, my dick was hard as a rock, and I didn't dare move.

Then she pressed herself hard against me, ending the press with a little grind, and I knew I had to wake her up. She didn't know what she was doing and if I let her continue, I'd be the biggest asshole on the face of the earth.

Holy shit.

She was gorgeous, unbelievable perfection. Every single nerve in my body was on high alert. I didn't know what I had done to deserve this but I was determined to figure it out so I could wake up this way every day. I was on fire for her, burning alive as my emotions whirled and skidded around in my brain while I tried to make sense of what had happened and decide what to do.

Slowly, I lifted my hands to her waist and tried to will my erection away before she woke up and noticed it. I assumed it would be rude to let her feel it, but who knew? This was an odd situation, to say the least.

My morning wood retreated after deep and thorough contemplation of every disgusting thing I could imagine. Several shallow breaths later and I was finally able to wake her up.

"Good morning, sunshine," I murmured, ruffling the top of her blonde head with my breath. Her hair had dried wild overnight, with waves spreading across my chest, much like the sunbeams shimmering in the light from the window.

"Morning," she mumbled, stirring against me and tightening her arms. "Where am I?" Her eyelids fluttered open, and she looked at me, studying my face in adorable confusion. "Liam?"

"Uhhh, we fell asleep at some point." I glanced at the coffee table, our plates and mugs were still there. "Probably after we finished eating. Pancakes and exhaustion don't mix well, I guess."

"Yeah, and that hot chocolate made me sleepier. I

guess warm milk isn't an old wives' tale after all. I'm making a note of that."

"Are you okay?" I whispered.

"Huh? Of course." She patted my pec. "I trust you, Liam. One hundred percent, okay? But we probably shouldn't have done this. Friends don't fall asleep all wrapped up together on the couch."

"Sure they do. Remember that old episode of *Friends* when Joey and Ross took a cuddle nap together? We were just two exhausted friends who crashed after a long night. I haven't slept this well in—well, ever, if I'm being honest. It's fine. You had a rough time, I had a rough time, and we were there for each other. Everything is okay."

"Are you sure? We're really okay?"

"Honestly? I'm rarely sure of anything lately. But what I am sure of is that it's Awkward Moments Day, so we're covered. Apparently, we inadvertently celebrated all night. Holiday hall pass for the win."

"God, you're amazing and clever and also surprisingly comfortable for a dude covered in rock-hard muscles."

"Don't forget relentlessly charming." I chuckled, gratified that she hadn't yet moved off me. She felt good where she was, and even though it was torture, I wanted to savor it.

"How could I forget about that? It might be my favorite thing about you."

"I'd offer you breakfast but . . ."

She patted my cheek then sat up. Amusement flickered in her eyes as she met my gaze. "Do you have coffee?

That's the one thing I can make and not screw up. Violet is my teacher, after all. I learned from the master."

"I do. Everything you need is in the cupboard near the sink. Have at it."

"Don't move, I'll bring you a cup. I know how you like it."

"That, you do." I sat and stacked our dishes from last night.

I heard her bustling around the kitchen. Soon enough the smell of coffee hit the air as it began to fill the pot.

She came back into the living room with her hair coiled into a low ponytail flowing over her shoulder. I missed those wild sunbeams that had covered my skin only moments before. I guess the little world we got lost in together last night had disappeared in the light of day.

"I'll take those." She collected the dishes and dashed back to the kitchen, returning a few minutes later with two mugs and a smile.

"Thank you. Do you have to work today?" I allowed myself one look at her long, gorgeous legs as she sat on the couch next to me. She must run a lot; they were sleek and toned to perfection. The memory of having my thigh in between them shot straight to my cock and I grabbed a pillow to cover myself, resting my arm across it to hide my reaction.

"Nope. Violet misses the shop so she's opening this morning. I'm going to check out Gram's old bed and breakfast. I assume Luke told you I'm opening an apothecary store with her?"

"He did. Congratulations, by the way. I think you'll

be great. I'm running the project—scheduling, permits, ordering what's needed, stuff like that. Owen is due to start the demo at the end of the week. Luke said you were okay with it, but—"

She waved a dismissive hand in the air. "Ew, Owen. It's fine, it was so long ago. I can't believe I was ever engaged to him." She seemed okay, maybe a bit annoyed.

"Are you sure you're okay? I'll say something if you're not."

"It's ancient history. Well, my feelings are ancient history. His wife is still determined to make me look like a combination of runaway bride and heartbreaking slut, though. But it is what it is. Luke feels sorry for him because they were friends when they were little. Plus one of his kids is in Dylan's class. I get it, it doesn't bother me. Luke is just a big softie."

"I'll be keeping my eye on him. Let me know if he steps out of line."

"I will. And look, I'm not as nice as Luke. If Owen didn't have, like, a million kids to support, I'd tell Luke to fire his ass and get someone else. And don't let get me started on his wife any more than I already did. I'm not above being petty when someone has crossed me."

"It's not petty at all. Your family is too nice," I muttered over the rim of my mug. "I *did* tell him to get someone else. In fact, I told Luke he should fire him. He's not a nice guy—there's something off about him."

She shrugged. "I'll be okay. Owen and his bullshit are the least of my worries. So, what are you up to today? Work? I've missed you at the shop, you know."

"Yeah? Work has been crazy. I've been having coffee early here at home. Uh—"

Her hand went to my knee. "I get it. I wish—never mind."

"Tell me."

"I wish I wasn't such a mess, is all. I make bad choices, Liam. I always jump into things I'm not ready for and end up screwing everything up. I don't want to do that anymore. It's hurtful. I want to be better. I mean, I have a plan and I'm taking steps and I'm, um . . ." Smiling, she threw her hands up, with a sharp-edged laugh. "How do you get me talking like this? One deep, growly, *tell me* and I start spilling my guts. Like I'm compelled to do anything you want me to."

I raised an eyebrow. If she were really compelled to do what I wanted, we'd be down the hall in my bed and I'd be buried inside her sweet little body right now instead of having coffee on the couch about to say goodbye for the day.

She flushed and I wondered if maybe my thoughts were obvious. But for once I wasn't sorry about not hiding it. I felt like the door that had been closed between us opened last night. Maybe it was just a crack, but it was big enough for me to get a peek inside and see the possibilities.

"I don't know what you're talking about. I'm just sitting here."

"Just sitting there. Sure, okay," she grumbled. "You're sexy in the morning and I think you know it. All gravelly voiced and rumpled up. Your hair is so cute all scruffy like that. I liked the buzz cut but this longer look you've got now is stupid hot. Damn it! Look at me. Spilling my guts again."

"Well, you're a ray of sunshine in the morning, and gorgeous too. And *I* think *you* know that," I teased.

Her cheeks flushed pink. "Hell yes, I am. My grumpiness is adorable, everyone says so."

"It's true, you're completely irresistible." It was taking every ounce of my willpower to keep from attempting to seduce her. To flatter and charm her into my bed with me, or hell, to lie her down on the couch, spread those long pretty legs of hers apart, and beg her for a taste of what had been warming up my thigh all night—

Stop it.

I had to put the mental brakes on before my dick punched a hole through this fucking toss pillow and I let her know exactly what having her this close all night did to me.

"We need another holiday, Liam," she whispered. "We both know if I kissed you right now, the last thing it would be is awkward and there's no pass for that."

"I'll find one. Next time I see you, you better be ready for it." We were playing with fire now, crossing the line between friendship and something else. But I wasn't about to stop now that she'd given me an opening to sneak through.

Her hand on my knee crept a bit higher. Did she realize what she was doing? Somehow, I didn't think so. "I like you, Liam, so much. This feels like the best kind of dare, and I want to be ready for it. You have no idea how bad."

I was earnest when I responded, "I get you more than you think I do, Holly. Please believe that. I'm not in the best place in my life either."

She drew her hand away to run through the end of her ponytail, letting out a low laugh when it got caught in the wild waves. "Maybe you do get me. I'm going to head down to Lily's place and scrounge around for something to wear home. Showing up at Jude and Levi's wearing nothing but your shirt and a pair of undies will give the wrong impression, and Jude has a big mouth. I tossed my leggings in your trash; I didn't even try to rinse them last night. I refuse to attempt whatever feat of laundry expertise would be required to get all that mud out."

"I don't blame you, they were wrecked. You took quite a spill. Are you doing okay? Does anything hurt? I have ibuprofen in the kitchen if you need it."

"I'm fine, nothing hurts. I think all that sleep helped. I kinda feel like a new person."

"Good, I do too. I wish I could sleep like that every night."

She smirked. "God, same. I'll see you later. Don't be a stranger at Vi's anymore, okay?"

"I won't." I held my fist out for a bump and she tapped it with a grin. "I promise."

"I'll hold you to it. Don't forget, I know where you work. I'll even show up at Mom's Sunday dinner to find you."

"Now I know you're serious. Take my hoodie, the one

hanging by the door. It's cold out there and it should be long enough to cover you up."

She snagged it and slipped it on, hugging her arms around her body with a grin. "I'll see you later, Liam. And I hope you know that I'll be keeping this hoodie too." She slipped into her shoes, waving over her shoulder as she rushed out the door, leaving me smiling on the couch.

She could steal my T-shirt, the hoodie too. Hell, she could take everything I owned. Why would I care about any of it when she was already so close to stealing my heart?

I ran my hands into my hair with a deep inhale and sank back into the couch. The sweet scent of her was all over me. I wanted to stay here and revel in the good feelings coursing through my body, but I had shit to do. I had to meet Jed at his ranch. My therapist recommended I volunteer out there, and I agreed that it would be good for me. Who wouldn't feel better being surrounded by service dogs and puppies all day? Maybe it would get her out of my head for a while.

Chapter 7
Holly

Hours later I was standing in front of Gram's old bed and breakfast, wondering if I dared go inside alone. The stately old Victorian sat at the edge of town, on the corner where you'd turn to head up to Luke's place. I could have jogged here if I'd wanted to, either down the road or on one of the forest paths. But since Lily had let me borrow one of her cars, I drove myself here instead.

The steps up to the door were rickety and as I got closer I could see how much work needed to be done. A simple coat of paint definitely would not suffice. The ornate details no longer highlighted the architecture, they aged it—like second day eyeliner on a partied-out face.

"There is no such thing as ghosts," I muttered to myself while twisting the not-quite-rusty key in the lock of what would eventually become our apothecary shop. After stepping inside, a quick glance at the darkness beyond the foyer made me leave the door open. Sunlight was required for this first visit. I was knee-deep in dust, old furniture, and some seriously haunted-house, Scooby-Doo vibes. A flicker of apprehension shot through me as I realized what a huge undertaking I'd agreed to.

Footsteps sounded behind me, and I smothered a shriek as I spun to find Lily and Gram crossing through the open doorway. "Oh my god. You guys!" Lily cried. "You can't open an apothecary store in here! No one will ever buy anything here if ghosts come as a bonus gift. Look at this place!"

"It's not haunted, you wuss." I didn't want to be alone in here, so I adjusted my position and grabbed her arm to keep her from running out on me. "It's just dusty and a bit run down, right, Gram? You never saw any ghosts when it was a B and B, did you?"

"No, never, not a single one. Calm your tits, Lily," she muttered as she moved around us, eyes roving over the state of the space as she walked. "Chillax, you two. It's fine."

"Gram!" Lily pretended to be shocked.

Luke snickered as he joined us in the foyer. "Yeah, baby, calm your tits."

She shot him a glare. "Whatever. I mean, look at this place! It screams haunted and is shrieking run-down hot mess. And I would not be surprised if someone dumped a body in here at some point. Do you smell that?"

"It is more run down than I thought it would be," Gram complained with a sigh. "I thought you cleaned up, Luke."

"No, that starts tomorrow," he told her. "It's going to be fine. Trust me."

"Good thing he's giving you two the family discount," Lily observed. "This place has enough dust to make an entire army of bunnies."

"There's nothing to worry about," Luke said. "I did a thorough inspection just like you asked. After a few minor repairs and the remodel, it'll be good to go. In fact, Holly, you can move into the top floor rooms in two, maybe three weeks if you want to."

"Really?" I perked up. I was dying to have my own space, though the thought of being alone here at night was freaky as hell.

"Absolutely. I have Owen scheduled to start work tomorrow morning."

"Not Liam?" Gram asked with a sly grin aimed my way.

"He's supervising. He's tied up helping me with another project at the moment. But don't worry, he'll be around to help once the demo is finished." Luke grinned back at her.

"Knock it off," I hissed at her when Luke turned around. "No matchmaking, remember? You're my safe space."

I didn't know Liam would be here "helping." What did "help" consist of anyway? The thought of being here while he worked made me shiver. He'd definitely be wearing a tool belt while he ripped up the carpet and knocked down the rear wall and all the other stuff on Gram's list. Every task would absolutely cause all kinds of flexing of his astounding musculature. What if he took his shirt off to work? I gulped.

No way.

I couldn't allow it to happen. My crush on him was desperate and pathetic, and completely out of control. Like, I was pretty sure I might have humped his leg a little bit in my sleep, but he was too much of a gentleman to mention it and I was a mortified mess, so like hell was I going to say anything about it.

Despite what I had told him this morning about not being a stranger, I just knew having to see him for more than a few minutes at a time would do my head the rest of the way in. I needed Vi's counter between us and a coffee shop full of people around or I'd tackle him clean off his feet and hump the rest of his body.

"Why can't you do it?" I asked Luke, trying to appear casual as Gram winked at me knowingly. "Shh," I mouthed at her.

"I have another project going on. I don't have the time, or I would do it myself."

"Okay. I see." I tapped my foot on the floor. I didn't want to ask for someone else to do the job. Luke was already giving us the family discount. Making demands would be rude. Plus, I didn't want to make Liam look bad by refusing to let him work here. I was so screwed. "I mean, I'm sure he'll do a great job." I didn't have a problem with him, I had a problem with *me*. Since the moment I first saw him, I'd been struggling to act like a normal adult woman and not a thirteen-year-old superfan locked in a room with their favorite boyband.

"Of course he will, Holls," Lily agreed. "He's awesome. It's going to be amazing and I'm happy for you. But I need to eat. These babies are stealing all my energy. I fell asleep in the car on the way here. Let's go to Vi's and get breakfast, Gram. Meet us there, Holly."

"I have to head off too," Luke said. "Owen will be here in about an hour to drop off the dumpster. I'm assuming you don't want to keep anything downstairs, right?"

"Right. Clear it all out," Gram confirmed. She welled up. "Looking around this place has made me nostalgic. I can't wait to see it up and running again. Grandpa would be so proud of you, Holly." She wrapped her arm around me and squeezed me in a cozy side hug. "You too, Luke. You know how much he always adored you. Thank you for helping me bring this old house back to life. She's got a lot of years still in her, don't you think?"

"Yeah, I do." He swiped a hand beneath his eyes as Lily hugged him around the waist. I'd noticed he had become quite sentimental after his return to Sweetbriar, but, then again, he'd always been a sweetheart. "I'm glad you're happy, Rosemary. It's my pleasure to help. And on that note, I have to get back to work."

"I'll see you later, sweetheart." Gram gave him a hug, then yanked him down to her short level to kiss his cheek. He waved goodbye and left. "Breakfast is my treat, girls. Let's get a move on."

We shuffled toward the door, and I wondered if I could get Jude and Levi to help me move in when it was ready before realizing all I owned was a couple boxes full of clothes and I should just do it myself. How sad was that? "I'll catch up with you. I want to look around a bit more. Check out the upstairs and maybe choose a room or something."

"We can wait for you." Lily offered.

"No. Go on to Vi's and feed those babies, Lil. I kind of want to be alone here for a little while."

Gram smiled softly. "Take your time, honey. Dream a little bit while you're here, it's okay. Grandpa and I used to love living here and I know you will too. Once the place gets cleaned up, of course."

"Yeah, and after we hold an exorcism and burn some sage to chase out the ghosts," Lily tossed over her shoulder as she left.

"Nice, Lily. Thanks for leaving me with that."

"I'm here to help!" she shouted. "Just not today . . ." Laughter flowed behind her, and I grinned, watching from the porch as she helped Gram into her car and drove off.

After stepping back inside and spinning in a circle I took it all in. Sure, it was a dusty, gross mess right now, but this house used to shine. It was massive but Gram had always made it cozy and homey and welcoming. I vowed to do the same.

I finally had my own place.

Step one to fixing my life. *Check.* Steps two to a zillion, ready to go. I should make a list.

Holly's De-fucking Up Her Life list.

I darted up the stairs. I knew exactly which room would be mine. The turret room has always had my name written all over it. Whenever I used to spend the night here with Gram and Grandpa, I always called dibs on it. I ran up the two sets of stairs, then continued up the spiral staircase that led to the top floor. Floor to ceiling windows covered every outside wall in the turret. I smiled huge as I recalled how much joy I used to get waking up with sunlight streaming over every surface of the room. It was almost as good as sleeping outside. There would be enough space for a bed and side table. I could keep the rest of my things—once I bought some things, that is—in one of the bedrooms next door.

Overall, I'd have my turret, two bedrooms, and two bathrooms on the top floor, which was more than enough space for me. The second floor was where the bed and breakfast guests had stayed; there were four huge bedrooms, each with their own bath, and a sitting area. The ground floor was where reception, dining, and the kitchen were located.

When we were done, I'd have the top two floors to myself, and the bottom would be fully renovated into the apothecary store. I was anxious to get into the backyard and start working on a garden—*my* garden. Shoving the curtains aside, I looked out over the yard, mentally planning where I would plant the herbs, flowers, and vegetables I was planning to grow.

"Holly Christine Barrett, we know you're still here. We saw you go inside!" I jumped at the sound of the voice shrieking at me from downstairs. "Get down here!"

Shit.

The voice belonged to Owen's wife, Ava, and I

guessed her best friend, Maren would be in tow. We'd gone all through school together since kindergarten. They had bonded over hating me and apparently, weren't done holding their petty grudges. Which was fair considering I hadn't let any of mine go either.

Owen was supposed to be here with the dumpster right about now. But instead, I was about to be graced with the presence of my one-sided small-town nemeses. This was the downside of small-town life. Your reputation always preceded you wherever you went and mine wasn't great for various reasons, only some of which were deserved.

I made it to the foyer to find them standing in the doorway. "What do you want?"

Ava's hands hit her hips as she glared at me. "What I want is to warn you to stay away from my husband, you home-wrecking skank. Owen is off limits."

"You know I'm no home-wrecker, Ava. Why are you really here?" The three of us had a few exes in common. Ava was now married to Owen, the ex-fiancé of doom. She was also with him before I was and blamed me for their breakup. Maren and I had unknowingly been involved with the same guy at the same time during our senior year of high school. Why she blamed me and not him for that, I did not know. Neither one of us had any idea what he was up to until it was all over, yet somehow, I had ended up the bad guy. They'd been spreading rumors and picking fights since. Obviously, nothing had changed while I was gone.

She stepped closer. "You know I don't see it that way.

He was about to come back to me before you stepped in. You stole him out from under me and then you broke his heart. Tossed him away like trash the day before your wedding." She raised a pointed finger in my direction and made a face I assume she thought was intimidating. "And I'm here to tell you, do not mess with my husband. Consider this a warning. Don't you dare try to tangle him up in your black widow web when he's over here working for Luke. I mean it, Holly. Don't even think about trying to hit on Owen and get him to go back to you."

I almost threw up in my mouth a little. "Gross, Ava. The only way I'd ever hit on Owen is with a bat, okay? He's a cheating, two-faced liar and a total creep. Now turn around and march your ass out of here before I make you." The other facet of my bad reputation was I wasn't afraid of a fight. The three of us, along with my best friend, Tess, had brawled our way all over this town before I left it. I was banned in every bar in Sweetbriar except for Holloway's and that was only because my aunt and cousins owned it.

"We aren't planning to stay and play catch up with you, honey," Maren interjected, her tone laced with faux sweetness. "We just needed to get a few things straight with you now that her man is working here, okay?"

"We do not have anything to get straight. We have nothing to say to each other. I'm not a home-wrecker or a man stealer. And Maren, really? Still? All this crap between us happened in high school. Move on. I have—"

"You got that right," Ava took another step toward me, wagging her pointed finger in my face. I fought the urge to break it off and poke her with it as she continued. "You sure as hell did move on! You dumped poor Owen at the altar, you bitch. I picked up the pieces. I was the one who put him back together but all he could talk about was getting you back—"

I threw my hands up in the air. "He was cheating on me, you idiot! Why would anyone want to marry a cheater? Especially one who would go crawling back to you the day after I left. I know the whole sordid story, okay? I dodged a bullet when it came to him. I feel sorry for you."

Ava looked ready to spit nails. "You're such a damn liar. You twist everything to make yourself look good."

"Whatever, Ava. Look, the only reason I'm not raising a stink about him working here is because you have kids to feed. But if you push me, I *won't* worry about your kids anymore, do you get me?"

"My god, you're so horrible, Holly," Maren accused. "I can't believe you'd use her kids against her like this."

"Typical Holly. Of course she's gonna hold my kids over me. But you need to understand something. Everyone in this town knows how you operate. You go from man to man. Taken or not, you don't care. What Holly wants, Holly gets, and we're sick of it. You should have stayed gone. Sweetbriar doesn't need the likes of you."

I bit my lip and kept my mouth shut.

Was what she said true? No.

But I understood why some people felt that way. On the outside looking in, it seemed like the truth. And instead of defending myself, I left Sweetbriar. It had been easier that way and I'd had better things to do with my life. My ambitions back then hadn't involved small town living. I still wondered why I had said yes to Owen's proposal when I'd known I had dreams to chase, places to see, and adventures to have. "I'm not talking about this anymore. You're both ridiculous. Get off my property."

"Fine, come on, Maren, we're leaving. But Holly, there's one more thing. Owen won't be here with the dumpster today. Unfortunately, he's sick." Her snotty grin made me want to knock it off her face, but I refrained because I was a fully grown adult now. I'd changed my ways, damn it. "Luke already knows."

"Oh yeah? Keep this shit up and Luke will know a whole lot more. Consider that my warning to you."

"Fine. Understood. But stay away from Owen." She whirled and stormed out.

"And don't even think of going anywhere near Jared." Maren added before she followed Ava out the door.

She was into Jared? Just freaking great. That wasn't going to bode well when it came to letting the drama between us die. Given his behavior the other morning, he was still into me. *Ugh!*

Reaching out, I slammed the door and locked it with a low scream. I shouldn't have come back to Sweetbriar. My thoughts whirled as I paced my way in an angry circle.

No. I'd been ready to come home.

If I wanted a life here, I either had to deal with all the high school and early-twenties bullcrap that was apparently going to follow me all the way into freaking eternity or let it go. Anyone I cared about knew the truth, so why should I care what a few small-town drama queens and their dumbass friends thought of me?

A knock on the door startled me out of my rage fest. Seething, I stomped through the foyer and threw it open. "What do you want now?" I growled.

It was Liam. Crap.

Startled, wide brown eyes met mine. "I, uh, saw two ladies drive off as I got here. I guess they're not your friends."

"Hey, sorry. Yeah, you could say that."

"Owen called out sick. I'm here to meet the dumpster." He laughed. "I mean, to sign for it and show them where to put it. Are you okay?"

"Yeah, I'm fine. Well, no, they ruined my happy planning-my-new-place mood and now I'm all tense and angry. The three of us have history. It's long, stupid, immature, and something I'd like to forget about but apparently that's not gonna happen. I have a past, Liam. My reputation around here is not the best . . ."

"Look, we all have pasts—"

I cringed. "Oh god, Luke probably told you all about me, huh? Probably warned you to steer clear of a mess like me."

"No. Well, actually, yes, but he didn't say anything specific. He told me anything bad I heard about you around town is bullshit and to pay it no mind."

"Oh, okay. I should have known better." Luke would

never believe lies about me. I'd known him since I was born, for eff's sake.

"Yeah, so turn that frown upside down, sunshine. You have nothing to worry about when it comes to me. Friends, right?" He held out his fist with a grin and I bumped it with a huge blush rising over my cheeks.

"I'll try not to worry."

"If anything, he probably warned you about me. I'm not great at the relationship thing. My track record at making things last is not the best."

"Yeah, but you were in the Army. How could you build something when you were gone all the time?"

He huffed out a laugh. "That definitely complicated things."

"You won't have that problem anymore, right?"

"I guess that's true."

"Do you want a relationship? A girlfriend? Wife?"

What the hell was I saying? STOP!

"Sure, someday. Do you?"

"Someday, yeah."

His voice turned velvety smooth as he said, "Interesting how we want the same things, isn't it?"

My mouth went suddenly dry. I had no idea how to respond. "Um . . ."

His phone pinged with a notification. He winked, letting me off the hook as he checked his messages. "The dumpster is around the corner. Let's meet them outside. We can get started on the clean-up together if you like."

"That would be awesome." I followed him to the porch. "I can't wait to move in. Luke said I could start in a few weeks, but I'd rather not live here when Owen is still working here. Plus, I need to save up for, well, everything. All I have is a few boxes of clothes and an old hairdryer."

"Good call. Don't move in until I get the locks changed and possibly new doors for the ground floor. I want you to be safe, so I'll put that at the top of my list."

"Thank you, Liam."

"Of course. So, I just came from dropping off the permit applications and plans. Your coffee shop friend Jared runs the office. Did you know that?"

I shook my head. "Ugh. I try to know as little about him as possible. No, I didn't."

Great, another likely dramatic complication that I didn't need in my life.

And now I was about to be alone with Liam again, a temptation that was getting harder to resist by the day.

Chapter 8
Holly

After our shared night of insomnia induced weirdness and the dumpster extravaganza of dust, old furniture, and too much information. Liam and I had fallen into a sort of rhythm. We had become great at small talk, innocuous flirting, and mildly provocative banter. Like, we knew we had shared feelings for each other, but we ignored them and stayed friendly. I was proud of myself every morning when I didn't hurl my body across Vi's counter to jump his sexy bones. I had the will of a freakin' nun, I did. And Liam? He managed to rein in his lady-killer charm like a champ. We were on a steady path toward friendship. It was a refreshing change of pace for me. I used to just dive right into everything without too much thought about it, but those days were over.

"So, how's it going at the inn?" Rose asked as I pulled a shot of espresso for her hazelnut latte. It was bright, way too early, and I was covering for Violet who had an appointment with her doctor this morning. I was behind the counter with Finn and Nick, Violet's teenage twins. They were out of school on spring break and my co-baristas for the morning. Gram was perched at a table up front enjoying scones and coffee while Rose waved manically at me as she approached from the front door. Lily was in the bathroom—again—since she was about a million months pregnant and had to pee every ten seconds.

"Good. I'll be moving in a couple weeks or so."

"I can't believe Luke is keeping Owen on after Ava went after you like she did the other day." She huffed as she placed her purse on the counter and I prepared her usual beverage of choice. "He needs to fire his dumb ass."

"Yeah, well, think of the children, Rose. That's what Luke is doing, and I don't blame him. Kids gotta eat. Chicken nuggets don't grow on trees, you know. And don't yell at him. I told him it was okay."

"And Liam? How's that whole thing going. Have you two banged yet?"

I spun around, almost spilling her latte. "What did you say, Rose?"

"Don't say bang in front of Finn and Nick, honey," Gram scolded from her table.

"Sorry, Gram."

"We've heard the word bang before, Gram." Finn snickered. "It's okay."

"There is nothing going on," I lied.

She shrugged and took a sip of her coffee.

Across the shop, I watched Lily shove her cell into

her purse and head up here. "Oooh, Holly almost spilled the coffee and Nick looks scandalized. What's going on?" She waddled as fast as she could to the counter, her ability to detect even the smallest hint of gossip still intact. I was impressed. "Did I miss something?"

"I was just asking Holly if she's managed to B-A-N-G it out with Liam yet. After all those hot eyes aimed at each other and the Valentine's Day make out session in the back room I figured it would be inevitable." Rose filled her in.

"We can spell, you know." Nick laughed at Rose. "Been doing it for years."

"We know where babies come from too," Finn added.

"Sorry, guys. We must be nothing but cringe this morning."

Finn's face transformed into an exaggerated grimace. "Kinda."

"Okay, listen." Lily checked her watch with a teasing grin and a flick of her wrist. "The . . ." She side-eyed Finn and Nick and mouthed the word *bang*. "Should be imminent, if my calculations are correct."

"What are you two freakshows even talking about? Liam and I are just friends. Yeah, we kissed but we both realized we aren't ready for more than that. And who I, uh, *hang* out with is nobody's business. Now be good and go sit with Gram, I have work to do. Violet will be here any minute and I can't let her see the mess I made back here."

"Too late, she's here and she sees all," Violet

announced grandly as she entered through the swinging doors that led from the back of the shop.

"That's just great," I groused. "How are you feeling? How's the baby?"

"Perfect. It's a girl. We're naming her Lyla, after Jake's mom. But enough about that. I could swear I heard the word bang. Who banged who? Tell me what I missed. Spill the tea. Boys, put your earmuffs on and go take a break while it's slow in here."

"Gotcha." They each grabbed cookies and drinks from the cooler, smirking as they headed to the back room.

The boys left and Rose did a brief scan of the shop. "Okay, we're clear," she announced. As if the customers filling the tables and chairs didn't have ears to eavesdrop with. "You missed nothing, Vi. As of now there is no banging to report," she whispered. "I'll lower my voice. I'm sorry, I should know better, I'm a teacher for eff's sake. Good thing there's no kids in here right now."

"Well damn. Come on, Holly," Violet encouraged. "I have good feelings about Liam, he'd be good for you. He's a solid guy and sweet too. He's a keeper. Go for it."

"Why are you all so sure I'm going to date Liam? And I refuse to say the word bang," I muttered. "Grow up."

"It's kind of a law, isn't it?" Lily held up a hand using her fingers to count down. "One, you've recently returned home to your small town. Two, you're fixing up a run-down inn with our nosy and adorable grandmother to turn it into an apothecary store—that's like double points, an inn and a store, don't you think?"

"Oh definitely," Rose agreed. "And three, her contractor is a super studly, yet somewhat fragile military veteran who is emotionally available, good with his hands—"

"I love this so much! All of it." Lily, losing what was left of her subtlety, clapped her hands together. "They'll be engaged before we know it. Do you want to shop for bridesmaid dresses after we have coffee?" She tugged on Rose's arm with a huge grin.

"Shut up," I mumbled, trying not to laugh at their ridiculous antics.

"When are you moving into the inn, Holly?" Rose didn't wait for an answer before blabbing to Lily again. "She'll be locked outside in a towel, or caught in the rain, or some other mildly dangerous and embarrassing thing he can rescue her from soon. It's just a matter of time." She shoved a finger in my face. "Get ready for it. The Hallmark laws of small-town living definitely apply to this situation."

I bit my lip as I remembered my mad dash through the forest the other night. "Seriously, you guys. Stop it." I couldn't let them find out he'd already rescued me from my self-induced panicked jog through the woods.

"Holly, tell me one thing," Lily looked me dead in the eye and I couldn't help but smile at her beaming face. "Have you noticed the lovely flecks of gold in his eyes yet?"

I turned red, I could feel the heat rise over my cheeks. Of course I'd noticed. Liam had the most gorgeous eyes I'd ever seen. Deep brown with long dark lashes, and yeah, the gold flecks were mesmerizing. I could stare into his eyes all day, damn it. "Oh god. Will you two give it a rest?"

"You're fine, honey. Don't pay them any mind. Leave your sister alone, girls," Gram scolded.

"Too bad he doesn't have a cute kid," Violet joined the madness. "Or maybe a dog or a cat. That's the one thing missing in this scenario. Something adorable we can *ooh* and *ahh* over."

Lily's phone pinged with a text. "Oooh, it's him. Perfect timing. Almost like it's fate or something." She winked broadly at me and waggled her eyebrows.

"I thought we were in a Hallmark rom-com, not a fated mates paranormal," Rose grumbled. "It's not fate if you text him, Lily. You are such a cheater."

"I don't care! Fate wants what it wants, and I want this to happen so I'm taking the actions needed to get this show on the road."

"This is perfect," I joked. "Let's switch to paranormal. Maybe some demented fairy king will sweep in and abduct me. I need someone to take me away from you three lunatics and I think I'd look good in a crown."

Violet raised her hand. "Hey, no way. I'd like to be recognized for my non-lunatic contributions to this conversation."

"Oh, come on," Rose laughed. "You know you love us."

"Of course, I do but you have got to cut this shit out. I'm trying a new thing. It's called not jumping into something I'm not ready for."

"And that's good," Violet soothed. "Right, you two?"

"You're on the right track, sweetie." Gram interjected. "Listen to Violet."

"Yeah, but—" Lily protested.

"There is no 'but,'" Vi insisted. "We all know Liam's your boy, Lily. It's like you've adopted him or something. It's nice, but also kind of weird. Isn't he older than you?"

"I'm protective," she defended herself. "So what if he's older? He's like a little brother to me anyway. I don't care if it makes sense or not. I want him to be happy and I acknowledge that I'm a bit pushy today. But Holly, you two are perfect for each other. You have to know it's true."

"Lily, I know he's amazing and wonderful and I like him—a lot. But I'm a mess right now and I won't pull him into that. I need to get settled, get my store going. Find my place here in Sweetbriar again. I still feel like I'm drowning most of the time, and I won't pull him under with me. I'll end up screwing everything up like I always do, and he deserves more than that."

"But—"

I held a hand up. "I'll be the first one in line if he's still available after I get my shit together, okay? I know how awesome he is, trust me on that."

"God, you're being so responsible and making so much sense," Rose grumbled. "Fine, be an adult. Boring, *ugh*."

"Um, thank you?"

"No, this is good." Lily shook her head. "You're totally right about me, I'm pushy and nosy and want everyone to be happy. I get it and I'll back off. I swear, I will. But it's too late for today because I already texted Liam to meet me here. I'm really sorry and I promise I won't push anymore. You're right, you deserve to move as fast or slow as you want."

"Well, thank you—"

"Plus, Luke might be a little bit mad at me. Well, not mad. He doesn't get *mad* at me. He thinks I need to mind my own business when it comes to Liam."

Gram approached the counter with her mug and by the look on her face to also drop some of her signature demented wisdom. "If he's upset with you, honey, text him a picture of your boobs and he'll forget all about your meddling. I need a refill, sugar pie, please."

I took her cup with a sideways grin. "You got it."

"Gram!" Lily's expression was a combination of horrified and trying not to laugh. "The last thing I need is for my boobs to end up on the cloud for Dylan or whoever else gets on our WiFi to find."

I laughed, noticing how she wasn't opposed to sending tit pics to Luke, just getting busted for it.

"They're just tits, Lily," Gram scoffed. "Get over yourself."

"Oh my god, Gram!" Rose burst out laughing.

"I don't get what you're all worked up about." She rolled her eyes. "You girls are such prudes. Isn't this supposed to be a new millennium? Why did I even bother burning my bras?" she scoffed. "Think of it as a memento of your sexy years. In my day we didn't have the cellular telephones and the internet. If I flashed my boobs at a concert, or Mardi Gras, or what have you, I would be lucky to get a polaroid out of it. And those were too easy to lose, especially if you were drunk." She shrugged. "I do have guitar picks and beads at home in my hope chest, but it's not the same. I had a nice rack, girls, and nothing left to remember it by. Learn from my mistakes and get photographic documentation."

She'd finally done it. We were all shocked silent.

"Okay, that's definitely a perspective," Violet finally said. "Uh, so back to the subject at hand. We're all going to back off and let Holly be, right?" They all mumbled their agreement, probably still too shocked by Gram to argue.

"What just happened? You're all agreeing with me?" I huffed a laugh. "It's okay. It's not that I want to avoid him. It's just, I can't even explain how I feel when I don't completely understand it myself."

"Hey, it's okay." Violet pulled me in for a hug and whispered in my ear. "Don't let them get to you. You know how they can be. They're easily excitable, like yippity little chihuahuas. I, for one, think you're making good choices and I'm proud of you. I'm here if you want to talk for real. They are too, you know that, right? You just have to push past the wackiness."

"Thank you and yes. I know they are. They just want me to be happy."

The front door *dinged*. Liam walked in.

Meow

Was that a cat?

My sisters and I exchanged a glance before the three of them burst out laughing.

It wasn't going to end now. I would just have to accept it. He had just entered with what had to be an *ooh*-able and *ahh*-able critter and judging by the bulge, it was stuffed into the pocket of his flannel shirt. Lily and her fate and her Hallmark movie matchmaking had just scored a point.

"Is that a cat I hear?" Gram spun to look.

"I was out at Jed's volunteering. I found this little guy in a wood pile up near the road when I was leaving. Cute, right?" He pulled a sleepy orange kitty from his shirt pocket, then tucked him against his neck where it proceeded to curl up against his beard and purr its fluffy little brains out. Kind of like what I'd probably done in my sleep. "Whoever dumped him there better hope I don't find them."

Did I just become jealous of a cat?

Why, yes. Yes, I did.

"Maybe it really is just a matter of time," Lily mused as a smug smile slid across her face. "Sorry, Holly. I don't make the rules. Hey, Liam."

"Hey, you needed me to meet you here, Lily?"

"Oh, yeah. Um, I'm sorry. It was a false alarm."

"You're okay? The babies are okay?" he asked, eyes full of concern. God, he really was so sweet responding to her random texts like this.

She nodded, clearly struggling to come up with an excuse to why she'd brought him out here.

"Come on, forget the coffee, Lil. Let's go dress shopping." Rose grabbed Lily's hand and off they went out the front door.

"What's that about?" Liam's bemused gaze followed them as they left before turning to me and Violet behind the counter.

"You never can tell when it comes to those two," Violet answered, covering for the weirdness that would ensue if she told him what we had been talking about.

"Are you keeping him?" I asked.

"Sure, why not? I could use the company, right? I miss having a cat around."

My eyes got huge. "You're a cat person?" Freaking damn it.

Fate, is that you?

"I'll cover the shop, Holly. The boys and I will close. Take the rest of the day off and help Liam get settled with his cat. I know you want to." Violet winked at me with a grin. She was the real master. I had been obsessed with cats since I was a little girl, a fact she was well aware of. The only reason I didn't have one or three or seven yet was because I didn't have my own place. Lily and Rose would never be able to compete with her. For Violet, matchmaking was organic. Damn she was good. So much for staying behind the counter when it came to Liam.

"Thanks." I stepped out from the counter already reaching for the cat. Liam handed him to me with a chuckle. "What are you going to name him?"

"I haven't decided yet."

"Oh, I know! Name him Chester. He's orange like a Cheeto. Or maybe Cheddar? Let's not forget about our shared cheese obsession—maybe we could commemorate it." Before our Valentine's Day kiss, we'd done some serious damage to a charcuterie board and discovered our mutual fondness for cheese of all varieties.

"I like Cheddar."

"Professor Cheddar Bartholomeow Chesterpaws. Do you have stuff for him yet? Litter box, food, bed, toys, catnip, treats, blankie—"

"Professor?" he questioned, gaze lowering to where I cuddled Cheddar to my chest.

"He seems kind of serious, don't you think? And it looks like he has a monocle." I pointed to his left eye, which was encircled by a white stripey ring.

"I guess so. He was seriously pissed about being abandoned in a wood pile at the side of the road. But I came straight here from Jed's to meet Lily. I have nothing for him yet."

"I got you. Follow me. My friend Tess owns the pet shop around the corner." I took his hand and dragged him behind me as I headed toward the door then shoved it open with my hip. "She'll get you all set up."

"I haven't met Tess yet." He held the door over my head, and I turned, flashing him a grin, no longer worried about jumping him now that we had this little kitty to take care of. Cat happiness trumped everything else as far as I was concerned.

"She's awesome. We've been best friends since kindergarten. Her sister Elizabeth runs the Quickbriar Stop-and-Go. You definitely know her, everyone in town does. Anyway, we don't hang out that much since I got back to town because her husband can't stand me. They have two kids but really, she's a single mom of three if you get what I'm saying. She told me he won't babysit so she can go anywhere with me. *Babysit?* His own dang kids?"

"That's awful—"

"Right? Anyway, he's a giant man baby—ever since high school. He's literally incapable of doing anything for himself. Like, she used to go through the line and bring him his freaking lunch tray, can you believe that? He was such a little turd. We used to beat each other up in second grade. But I'm working on control and acceptance. So far, I've managed not to shit talk him to her face. So please don't repeat anything I just said."

"Wow." A deep chuckle rumbled behind me as we walked. "I won't repeat a word, I swear."

"Sorry." I cringed. "The more comfortable I get around you, the more useless information is gonna come tumbling out of my mouth. I'll try to rein it in."

"Don't be sorry and don't rein anything in. It's cute as fuck."

I stopped short on the sidewalk. Red faced and flustered as I turned to him. "What?"

He touched a fingertip to my nose. "You're adorable."

"Oh." A nervous laugh burst out of my mouth. "You're not so bad yourself, and I might steal this cat to go along with your T-shirt and hoodie. Professor Cheddar needs a mommy to cuddle, doesn't he?" I cooed, kissing the top of his furry little head. I shrugged my shoulders, embarrassed even though he said I was cute. The hoodie slipped off my shoulder.

He straightened it, eyes burning into mine. "If you need something to cuddle while you're wearing my clothes, I'm happy to volunteer. I'll even bring Cheddar with me."

"You're a cuddler?" I slammed my eyes shut against his knowing smile.

"That's something you'll have to discover for yourself. First-hand information is the best kind."

"Ahh, I'm intrigued. And you'll discover—quite easily, I might add—that I let it all hang out through rambling bursts of *too much* information. I'm an open book. It's a character flaw."

He looked down at me, lips tilted up at the corner. I could see the invitation smoldering in the depths of his gorgeous brown eyes. "As far as I'm concerned, you're flawless."

With one word, I could discover *everything* about him and ramp up our friendship to something more. It was written all over his face clear as day.

Chapter 9
Holly

"Please tell me it's cat appreciation day or something?" I was breaking all my rules and I needed a reason. I wanted to spend the rest of the day with him picking out the essentials for Cheddar and easing him into his new life as a cat dad. Honestly, I wanted to spend the rest of the day with him anyway, cat or no cat. I had no reason other than I liked him. A lot. He was fun and sweet and adorable and sexy, and I was pretty sure I could fall for him if I let myself. But my days of reckless abandon were over so I couldn't. Not yet.

"Nope, sorry. It *is* Waffle Day though. Want to stop for chicken and waffle tacos at the food trucks on the way back to my place?"

"Um, heck yes, I do. Those are my favorite. Holiday hall pass!" I held my fist out and he bumped it with a grin.

"It's also Tolkien Day," he informed me. "I hope you're ready to find out what a huge fantasy nerd I am."

"Uh, dude, *The Hobbit* is my favorite book of all time and I watch at least one of the movies a week with Jude and Levi. Wanna watch a movie tonight too?"

"Absolutely. You're becoming one of my favorite people to spend time with, Holly." A smile tipped up the corner of his mouth before he turned to put the bags in the truck, then opened the passenger door for me. "I'll get the rest. Be right back."

"Okay." I sat the cat carrier on the seat and took Cheddar out to snuggle him.

"Holly." The deep voice close to my back made me jump. "Did you get a new truck?"

I whirled and poor Cheddar let out an alarmed meow. "Jared." I was only a tiny bit relieved it was him instead of a pickpocket or carjacker. "Don't sneak up on me like that and no, it's not my truck."

"I'm sorry. I didn't mean to startle you."

"Sure, it's okay." I tucked Cheddar closer to my chest.

"I received your permits today. An apothecary shop, huh? Looks like you'll be staying in Sweetbriar after all."

"That's the plan."

"You know about the Sweetbriar Street Festival, right? The Sweetbriar Chamber of Commerce, which I happen to be on the board of"—he winked at me—"holds it every year. We started the tradition when you were gone, and I've never seen you attend one so I'll explain. Local shop owners set up booths for the town folk and other business owners to sample their wares. There will be live music, a dance floor, kid games . . . you name it, and we have it. You should plan on setting up a booth. It would be a great way to get the word out about your little store. You can have a booth even if it's not officially open yet, just fill out the papers. I'd love to be your official escort. I could introduce you around. There will be suppliers in attendance as well as merchants. It would be a great way for you to make useful contacts."

"Uh, I don't—"

"I'm trying to be a nice guy here." He grinned. "Cut me a break, will you?" His voice was teasing, even flirty, but it left me cold. "Anyway, did I mention I'm about to put you on the schedule for the inspection of your building? Next week, perhaps?"

"No, I wasn't aware of that. Luke and Liam are running the renovation. They're supposed to take care of everything. You should probably contact one of them—"

"Of course. Luke's company is always above board on everything they do. Owen is a worry, though I'm sure you know all about his reputation around town. I'd hate for anything to get in the way of you opening your store . . ." He was hinting at something but I had no idea what it could be.

"Right . . ."

"So, about the Sweetbriar Street Festival? I'll shoot you a text or stop by Violet's to make plans. Yes?"

"Sure, we can talk about it later." Was he threatening my permits in order to get me to go with him? I dismissed the thought. He wouldn't do that. *Would he?*

Liam approached with the rest of Cheddar's things and dumped the boxes into the back of the truck with a borderline hostile look aimed at Jared.

"Hey. What's going on?" His face was stone, and his voice was growly and pitched intimidatingly low. If I didn't know him, I'd be scared right now.

Jared spared him a glance then nervously cleared his throat. "Cute cat, Holly."

"Yeah, thanks. It's Liam's." I wanted to put Cheddar back in his carrier. I didn't want him anywhere near Jared, which was a weird thought, but I also didn't want to turn my back on him, which was an even weirder thought.

"Hey, remember that cat you had back in high school? Persephone, was it?"

I nodded without answering. She was the most beautiful kitten I'd ever seen. My mom had rescued her from an animal shelter. She was an early birthday present a few weeks before I turned sixteen. She had disappeared sometime during my birthday party. I had spent weeks looking all over town for her and Jared had insisted on following me around and helping.

"We spent all those weeks together, putting missing posters up all over town. It broke my heart how sad you were."

"I remember."

Liam didn't say a word. He just watched, glaring at Jared as he tried to get a conversation started with me before finally giving up.

"Well, I have to run. Business to attend to—you know how it is. Don't forget about the Sweetbriar Street Festival, Holly. We'll chat about it later."

"Okay. Bye."

We watched him walk away. "I do not like that guy. Something is off about him," Liam finally said as he helped me into his truck and shut the door.

I didn't either, to be honest. And now it seemed like he was going to be a problem. I got the feeling he had expectations when it came to me, and I didn't like it one bit.

I let out a sigh.

"Is everything okay? Did he say something to upset you?"

I hesitated. "No. He's fine, just a bit overeager. I can handle him. I've been doing it for years."

He looked at me doubtfully. "Let me know if he gives you any trouble. Big or small, it doesn't matter, say the word and I'll step in. The offer still stands."

"Thanks, but I'm fine." A change of subject was imperative. Liam was giving off major protective vibes and I couldn't have him jumping the gun and going after Jared. I decided to keep the questionable nature of our interaction to myself for now. I had no proof he was threatening me other than how I had felt. And I couldn't trust that anymore, not when everything made me suspicious and I was so easily spooked.

"Would your smile come back if we forget about that prick and got back to Waffle Day, Tolkien, and cat stuff?" His lips turned up at the corner as he started the truck.

"Yes, definitely." I smiled, relieved he was letting the run-in with Jared go.

He pulled out and drove us to the food truck lot, then to his place.

Three trips from the truck to the house later and we'd unloaded all of Cheddar's new stuff. "I went overboard." Liam scanned the pile of boxes and bags with a frown. "He's a baby, he doesn't need a six-foot cat tree."

"Sure he does. He needs to set goals for himself, Liam. Think of how he'll feel when he finally climbs to the top."

"Okay, you could have a point there. But I'm not setting up the water fountain yet. What if he falls in?"

"That's a good call. Wait on that."

"I bought too many toys. And is catnip really good for cats? Isn't it the equivalent of giving him drugs? Maybe I'm spoiling him? I don't know about all this. My grandmother took care of our cats. All I did was pet them and let them sleep on me."

I found myself caught up in a fantasy of sitting on his lap while he stroked my hair. I would definitely purr if he did that. I blinked the image out of my head.

Focus, dummy. Waffle Day is not an excuse to act like an idiot. Holiday hall passes are not a real thing, no matter what you keep telling yourself. Feelings are real and can be way too easily hurt.

Back to the task at hand. I got hold of myself. "You have nothing to worry about. Tess is an expert. She almost became a veterinarian, but dumbass got her pregnant and she dropped out of college and opened the pet shop instead."

His eyes flicked to mine in disgust. "I do not want to meet him."

"Dude, I wish I didn't know him. But forget about all

that. You're going to be a great cat dad. Look at how much he already loves you." Cheddar was curled up against Liam's neck and I was once again jealous of a freaking cat. "You rescued him from a wood pile. You're his hero."

He chuckled. "That's a bit of an overstatement, but I'll take it. I'll be fine. Just food, water, and a litter box to take care of, right?"

"Exactly. And the most important part—you already love him. I can tell."

We unpacked enough stuff for Cheddar to be comfortable, leaving the cat tree and most of the toys for Liam to deal with later.

Now we were sitting on his couch with *The Lord of the Rings* playing on the TV and chicken and waffles on the coffee table ready to eat as we watched Cheddar wear himself out running circles around the rug.

"I love this." I tilted my head to the side and stole a look at him. I was relaxed. I was at ease. I hadn't felt either in a long time.

He slid his hand along the couch and covered mine. "What do you love? Tell me."

My cheeks heated. I was the queen of too much information and giving myself away, but Liam felt safe, so I went with it. "Making friends with you. Getting to know you better. I never do this. I always jump in headfirst to uh, dating, friendships, everything really, and mess it all up. You're different. You're too—"

"Too what?"

"Too important to lose. I like having you around, Liam."

"That's good because I like being around you."

"Okay, then I'll quit worrying that I'll freak you out and drive you away with my indecision, hesitation, and crushing doubts. Not to mention my rambling and propensity toward giving too much information." Occasionally when I started feeling close to someone, like a new friend or a potential love interest, I would overshare my feelings. And once I started, I had trouble stopping. This was turning into one of those times. "I have lost all perspective. I like you more than I'm ready for and I don't know what to do about it. *Ugh!* Let's watch the movie, and eat the food, and I'll stop talking now." Blood pounded in my temples when I realized what I had confessed to him. My face was in flames, I could feel it. I also felt his eyes on me and I wanted nothing more than to disappear into the couch cushions or dive out the window.

"Holly, hey." With those two words, his voice seemed to echo my own longings, but I still couldn't make myself face him.

I shook my head. "What?" I whispered, suddenly watching Cheddar's kitty cat zoomies around the coffee table were of the utmost of importance and I couldn't possibly look away.

"Will you look at me? Please?"

"I don't think I can. If I do, you'll discover exactly how bright the color red can be once you get a peek at my cheeks. I talk too much, Liam."

"No. You don't. I love talking to you. Every conversation with you is like sunshine lighting up my day, Holly. Please believe that. I'll be your friend forever and if you tell me you want something more someday, believe me when I say I will listen because I'll want it too. I already do. How's that for too much information?"

I peeked at him from the corner of my eye and watched the emotions play across his face. "Really?" He was sincere. It was written all over his face.

"Absolutely."

"I'm not driving you crazy or leading you on?"

"You can't lead someone on when you explain yourself as thoroughly as you do. It's not possible. I know where you stand and honestly, I'm right there with you." I opened my eyes, turning fully toward him to look into his steady gaze. He cupped my chin and leaned forward to kiss my forehead. "The waffles are getting cold, and Cheddar is staring at us." The warmth of his smile echoed in his voice, putting me at ease again.

Meow

"I guess we'd better eat then."

"Get comfortable and dig in. I have a progress report for you."

"Yeah?"

"Yup. You have steel doors with new locks and a state-of-the-art alarm system. You can move in next weekend after Owen finishes hauling the old stuff away and Luke and I knock down the back wall."

"Seriously?" I threw my arms around his neck, tackling him backward on the couch. "You are awesome."

His eyes flickered with amusement as he pulled me into a hug. "It's my job."

"I won't get in the way while the renovation is happening?"

"No, and you won't be there alone with Owen, so don't worry about that. I'm going to be hands on once the renovation begins. I'll be there every day, full time, until it's done and you're ready to open. He's just on trash and floor duty."

"I can't wait."

He chuckled. "I know, that's why I lit a fire under Owen's ass. That and to get him out of your space quicker."

"You're the best. I have barely any stuff to move in, and I don't even care. Air mattresses are cheap, right?"

"I don't think you'll have to worry about that." He winked. "But that's all I can say. I've been sworn to secrecy."

My eyes lit up. Call me a kid, but I loved surprises. "I can't wait even more now."

Chapter 10
Liam

Tolkien and waffles had been about week ago. It was now Tell a Lie day, which was appropriate since the lies I had been telling myself for months about my feelings for Holly were now totally out of control. Despite my attempts to keep some distance between us, I was completely addicted to how I felt when I was with her. She made me feel alive. She made me hopeful. I was finally able to contemplate my future and expect it to turn out happy someday.

But she wore her heart on her sleeve and I knew it wasn't ready for me and my feelings for her. She didn't hide it. Subterfuge and manipulation were not in Holly Barrett's arsenal of considerable weapons. In fact, her extreme honesty is what I liked the most about her, even if the things she said weren't necessarily what I wanted to hear. I was done being with women I had to figure out. I had no time for games and the fact that Holly didn't play them attracted me to her like a magnet.

She was moving tomorrow. Owen had finally cleared the remaining debris and Luke and I were here to knock out the wall that separated the dining and living rooms so the space could be wide open for the transformation from inn to apothecary shop.

Sledgehammer in hand, I took a whack at the wall, satisfied at the soft crunch as I pulled it out along with a huge chunk of plaster.

"You're quiet today," Luke observed before taking his own swing at the wall. "Is everything okay?"

"What? Yeah, I'm fine."

"Okay. Well, maybe I'm not." He took another whack then faced me with a challenge in his eyes.

I set down my sledgehammer and turned to him. "What's happening? Everything okay with Lily? The babies? Are Dylan and Calla all right?"

"Yeah, that's not it, everyone's fine. It's me. I promised your grandmother I'd stick with you and I feel like I'm failing at that. I know something has been on your mind lately. Are you missing her? Is that it? You can talk to me about it. I won't check out on you again, I swear."

Years ago, after Luke and I had become friends, he started joining me on leave whenever I'd visit my grandmother. In the end he was almost as close to her as I was, and she had treated him like he was another grandson.

"You didn't check out on me and yeah, I miss her all the time. I think she held on for so long so I wouldn't be alone. I thank god I had her for those first few months after we got back. She was all both of us had when we were enlisted. You're grieving her too, and that's probably something we should talk about more."

"The last day I saw her, in the hospital, I promised her we'd both be okay, that I'd stick with you, take care of you. But I feel like I failed at that, and I haven't told you how sorry I am for how I handled things the day she died. I should have known how hard it would be for you, but I ran home and hid instead."

"What? No. No way. What I did was not your fault. You saved my life, Luke. Hell, you did it twice, don't forget that. I'd be dead if you hadn't hauled my ass to safety and who knows what would have happened if you and Lily hadn't showed up at my place that day." The day I was still trying to wrap my head around. The day I came to my senses drunk with a gun in my hand and no memory of how it got there or what I had been planning to do with it. I was determined not to fall to that depth of despair ever again.

I remembered feeling like I had no one left. I was the last living member of my family. When my dad died, I had my mother and grandmother. When Mom died, I still had my grandmother. She picked me up from school and I spent the night at her house like it was any other day. She didn't tell me about my mother until morning. It would be better if I found out in the light of day, she'd said. She wanted to be with me while I processed the fact that I'd never see my mother again. When she died, I found out from her doctor over the phone and I was alone.

"But it wasn't me who saved you, it was Lily. She

busted into my house and forced me to open my eyes. I was stuck in my own grief, my own sense of failure and loss. She saved both of us." His voice was little more than a broken whisper, but it packed a punch. I had never been alone, not really. And I didn't have to keep feeling like I was now. "Fuck, Liam, I'm glad you're still here."

I blinked back emotion as I contemplated what could have happened if he and Lily hadn't showed up for me. "So am I, Luke."

"I really don't know what I'd do without you."

"I'd hug you, but I'm covered in plaster and dry wall dust."

"Fuck it, I am too." He tugged me into him, slapping my back before letting me go again.

"I guess I should buy Lily flowers or something. You know, for pulling your head out of your ass. That couldn't have been easy." I had to crack a joke. The two of us together could get overly maudlin and sentimental since we'd come home and had started getting help.

"Nah, man." He chuckled, wiping his eyes with his dusty sleeve. "Get her a lemon cream pie, or a box of chocolates, or a side of beef. Food is where it's at these days. Growing those twins has her eating more than I do. It's amazing."

"I'll make her a batch of my mom's chocolate chip cookies. How about that?"

"I'll try not to steal any. Oh, guess who's learning to bake? Holly and Rosemary were at the house the other day." I lifted my eyebrows and waited for him to answer. "She has Rosemary teaching her how to bake snickerdoodles. If she gets it right, make sure to steal some of those. They're great."

"I'll keep that in mind."

He looked at me. "So, you're really okay?"

"Yeah, and you should know. We talk about everything in Jed's PTSD group every week." I smirked at him. "You know how I can't shut up there."

"You're right." He rubbed the back of his hand across his brow. "Maybe I'm letting guilt eat at me."

I clapped my best friend on the shoulder. "You have nothing to be guilty for, Luke. And I don't either. The past is in the past and we're moving on and up and forward, all of it. Everything."

"You're damn right we are. All right, Let's haul the rest of this shit out. The furniture delivery should be here any minute." We were finishing the last few steps of demolition work before the renovation started at the inn. Owen would start painting the exterior at the beginning of the week while I'd begin on the interior.

We were also here to supervise the delivery from the furniture shop in town. They were coming here to set up Holly's new place. Her siblings had gotten together and ordered her a bed, a living room suite, and everything she'd need to live here and be comfortable. I'd bought her a surprise of my own that was waiting for her upstairs. I hoped it wasn't too much.

They were planning to surprise her after dinner tonight. Holly had missed the last few Barrett Sunday dinners. I was curious what they'd told her to get her to come tonight.

"Sometimes I wish I had a big family like this growing up," I mused.

"I get it, I feel the same way sometimes. But neither one of us is alone—we have each other. And let's face it, we have the Barretts too. Try to miss Sunday dinner and see what happens." Luke slapped me on the shoulder, then bent to grab the broom to sweep out the remains of the wall we'd just torn down.

"Good point." The Barrett family was nosy and always up in each other's business, but that's what made them great. The way they always rallied around each other was a beautiful thing and the fact that they'd taken me in like one of their own was something I'd always be grateful for.

A few hours later, after going home to clean up and change, I was pulling into the long winding driveway to the Barrett family property. Like Luke, they lived in the country. Their home was a massive white ranch house that had been added onto over the years to the point it sprawled awkwardly in every direction, but still managed to be cozy and homey despite its size. The driveway was paved in old brick and wound around over the fifty or so acres they owned. I cruised up to a low fence that edged what could be considered a backyard amidst the vast property and parked. I got out of my truck and headed for the house, smiling as a bubble popped on my forehead and I heard kids talking on the other side of the fence.

"She's not a real grown up." It was Dylan's voice.

A peek over the fence showed Holly sitting cross legged on the lawn surrounded by the little kids of the family ranging in age from kindergarten to about second grade. I stopped with a grin and stood there listening and wishing I could have had a childhood as simple as this. Blowing bubbles without a care in the world.

"I think you're a secret kid, Aunt Holly," Maddie, Rose's stepdaughter lisped in her cute little girl voice.

"No she's not," Mikey, her older brother scoffed. "She's too big to be a kid."

"Oh yeah?" Holly's sweet voice rang out. "What if I am? What if I didn't want to grow up so I went on adventures all over the world instead?"

"That does sound amazing," Mikey grudgingly agreed. "I guess you can hang out with us. You brought bubbles and Skittles and that was pretty cool. But you're not a kid."

"Thanks, Mikey."

"Well, I still can't beat her at Mario Kart, and I've beat every adult in this family 'cept for her," Mark said. He was the son of Asher, the eldest of the Barrett siblings.

"She steals all the Peeps at easter. Every year, no Peeps for the rest of us," Mara, Mark's sister added. "Kids steal candy. Adults can buy it at the store."

Holly laughed as they began listing all the evidence proving she was a big kid.

"Good, 'cause Peeps are 'scusting."

"Disgusting, Dylan?" Holly pulled him onto her lap and tickled him. "More like delicious."

"Ew. No, they make my tummy mad." He laughed as she let him go.

"They make mine mad too," Holly conceded. "But it's worth it, especially for the purple ones."

"Did you sit at the kids table for breakfast because you don't have a husband?"

"Ouch." Holly burst out laughing. "That was way harsh, Mikey."

He shrugged a shoulder with a hilariously jaded grin. "I keep it real."

"I guess I can respect that. But maybe I sat with you guys because I like you. You're more fun to talk to. No talking politics, no relationship stuff, no one trying to fix me up or ask me why I'm not dating anyone. Plus, you had tiny pancakes at your table and my mom gave you sprinkles to put on top. So, how about that?"

"Well." Maddie peered up at her. "Why don't you have a boyfriend? You're really pretty and I like your hair. You're funny, too—"

Mikey cut her off. "She's even scared of the dark like you, Maddie."

"How did you know that?" Holly asked him.

"The last time we all spent the night here, when you first came back, your light was on all night."

"You're very observant."

"My dad says I'm nosy. When I grow up, I want to be a police detective like him."

"That's not a bad idea. I think you'd be great at it."

"We're not your real niece and nephew, you know." Mikey was testing her. It reminded me of the way I had been with my grandmother when she first took me in after my mom died. Hesitant and suspicious, even though deep down I had known better.

"Who told you that?"

He shrugged and gave her a side-eye.

"There's only one solution. Come on, you two, bring it in. But only if you want to. No pressure to hug, ever. We can high five it out instead if you want." She opened her arms and waited, lighting up with a huge smile when they scooted into her hug. "Do I feel fake to you?" She pulled them close and kissed the tops of their heads. "Because you sure feel real to me. Listen, sharing the same blood is not what makes a family. Love does, and I love you guys, okay? Just the same as I love Dylan and Calla and Mark and Mara and Finn and Nick, and the future new babies from Violet and Lily, okay?"

"M'kay. I love you too, *Aunt* Holly." Maddie wrapped her arms around Holly's waist and squeezed while sticking her tongue out at Mikey. "She's real, Mikey. I told you so the other day. *Duh.*"

"I was just making sure. A guy can't be too careful, you know? You can't just love everyone, Maddie, you could get your feelings hurt."

"I shouldn't have missed so many Sunday dinners," Holly told them. "Then you would know exactly how I feel. I'm sorry, you guys, I won't stay away anymore. You're a wise kid, Mikey. It's good to be careful with your heart."

"It's okay. I forgive you and I know it's wise. Being careful is important," he said in a voice that sounded much too old for a kid his age. "I grew up too fast. I have therapy about it every week."

"I had therapy too." Holly murmured. "It's good to talk about your troubles with people who can help you."

I froze. *Troubles?*

"What did you have therapy about?" Dylan asked. "Grandma said you almost got hurt before you came home. Is that why?"

"Yes, that's why. Uh, it's kind of scary. I don't know if I should tell you about it."

"I know what happened." Mark said. "A bad guy got into your tent when you were hiking, that's what I heard my dad say when he was talking to Grandpa." His face paled. "Oh no, they said I wasn't supposed to ask you about it."

"You're gonna get in trouble now." Mara's eyes were huge.

"It's okay, nobody is getting into trouble," Holly soothed. "You didn't ask me anything, did you?" Her voice was gentle as she reached out for Mark's hand.

"No, but I talked about it, and I didn't mean to. I don't want you to be mad or sad or feel something bad. I'm sorry."

I held my breath while I waited to hear her response.

"Don't worry, sweetheart. We can talk about it, it's okay. I was on a hike up the Pacific Crest Trail and I woke up with a strange man breaking into my tent. He wanted to hurt me, but I didn't let him. So don't worry, I didn't get hurt and I'm okay. But it scared me pretty badly, so I came home right away. Luckily, I was close by."

Had he hurt her, and she didn't want to tell the kids?

I recalled the first time I saw her, the day she had arrived back to Sweetbriar. Not a mark on her, no cuts, no bruises.

What had she done?

"That would be so scary. I'm glad you're okay."

"Thanks, Maddie. I'd much rather wake up to a stray cat in my tent, or even a rabbit. One time I woke up with three snakes curled up on my feet. I think they must have been cold. Now *that* was really scary. But I held still until they slithered away, and everything turned out okay."

"Ew, I hate snakes!" The kid chorus of *boos* for snakes made me laugh out loud.

Holly heard me and turned around. "Hey, Liam. We're just talking about some of the critters I've found in my tent over the years. Come on over and sit with us."

Dylan piped in. "Liam is my uncle but he's not my dad or mom's brother. So you don't have to worry, Mikey, see? Aunt Holly is right, she's your aunt and Liam can be your uncle, just like he is to me."

I cleared my throat as I sat down. "That's right. The family you choose is just as important as the one you're born into, sometimes even more."

"I know." Mikey patted my shoulder. "Dylan told us you're just like Luke. No more parents left at all."

"Are you like, an orphan or something?" Maddie asked me.

"Yeah, I guess I am."

"We can be your family too. Just like Dylan," she declared. "We have lots of new aunts and uncles now since our dad married Rose. She told us that love is all you need. She says it all the time."

Mikey reached his hand out for a high five. "We can exchange Christmas lists next Sunday. But Maddie and me are kids so don't expect too much."

"Well, thank you," I chuckled.

"I made macaroni necklaces last year for my dad and grandma. Do you like those?" Maddie asked.

"I love them."

"We should hang out more when you're here on Sundays." Mikey mused. "You're kind of cool. How do you feel about playing catch?"

"It's one of my favorite things to do," I told him.

"Yeah, Liam is cool," Dylan chimed in. "If he lifts you over his head, he's so tall it's almost like flying."

"Dinner is ready! Come on, kids!" Rose's voice rang out from the front porch.

"Heck yes! It's spaghetti Sunday and I can't wait. We'll talk more about the uncle, nephew, and niece stuff next week." Mikey hollered over his shoulder as he darted off like a shot followed by the rest of the kids.

"That kid is something else. Rose was not kidding." Holly laughed.

"Are you okay? I didn't mean to eavesdrop. I got caught up listening to them being so cute then it got serious. I'm sorry I overheard."

"I thought you might have." Her eyes drifted across

the yard. "Don't be sorry, it's not like it's a secret or anything."

"I'm here if you want another ear."

"Thanks, maybe I'll take you up on that. But not on spaghetti night." I knew her well enough by now to know she was joking to cover up her emotions.

"Okay, deal." I stood and held a hand down to her to help her off the grass.

She took it with a grin. "Have you heard? Tonight is the night. Me, my two boxes of clothes and my trusty sleeping bag are moving in."

"Yup, I heard. I was there with Luke earlier knocking down a wall to clear space for the shop. You'll have your own place, it's going to be great." Her life would start falling into order.

Would she still be interested in me?

"I hope so." Her pretty eyes locked to mine as a small smile tipped her lips up.

"Holly, I have a feeling you're going to have everything you ever wanted."

She linked our fingers and swayed close. "Since I got back to town, I found myself wanting more than I ever thought I would. It's been a long time since I've felt anything like this."

"Like what?"

She took my hand and placed it in the center of her chest without answering. Her heart raced beneath my palm as her smile flickered and faded.

I pulled her in for a brief hug. "I feel it too."

Chapter 11
Holly

Me, my two boxes of clothes, and my trusty sleeping bag were ready to go. After dinner with the family, Levi and Jude drove me to their place to pick up my things. They insisted on driving me over, joking that they'd each carry a box for me and help me set up camp upstairs.

Jude pulled into the driveway and cut the engine. "Here we are."

"We're gonna miss having you around." Levi was melancholy. "It was almost like back when we were kids —fighting over the bathroom, pizza Fridays, binge watching *Lord of the Rings* movies, beers on the patio . . . I mean, we don't have to steal them from dad anymore, but you get the idea."

"I'll miss you guys too, but it's not like I'm leaving Sweetbriar this time. You can always come over here for beer on the patio and *Lord of the Rings*. I'll even let you hold the remote while we argue over which of the movies to watch."

He turned to me with a smile and a heavy sigh. "But it won't be the same, Holls. Not if you *let* me hold it."

I let out a laugh. "Fine, we can fight over it. Then you can raid my most-likely-to-be-empty fridge."

"Promise to at least have a crusty jar of mustard in there," Jude chimed in. "I'll bring one of ours by next time."

"This will never truly be a home without one. I appreciate it and I love you guys for letting me crash with you for so long."

"We love you too, Holls."

"And, uh, you can come back to our place any time." Levi's offer was somehow both earnest and hesitant. "You know that, right?"

"What?"

"You can come back and stay with us. Whenever you need to, and it doesn't matter for how long."

My eyes narrowed. "Why do you think I'll need to?"

"Because of, you know, all that happened before you came back. All I'm saying is you can call one of us, and we'll pick you up. Or we can crash here with you. That's all I meant."

"Oh, okay." I mulled Levi's words over. "You don't think I can be alone here?"

"I didn't say that. I'm throwing it out there, just in case."

"All right." I wasn't offended. They knew some of what had happened to me. They probably noticed how I slept with the living room lights on too. How could they not? "I'll keep it in mind. I really want to move past what happened though. I'll be okay."

"Of course you will." Jude said, shooting Levi a *shut-up* look. "Let's get you settled in upstairs."

They exchanged yet another look as they opened their doors, though I couldn't decipher it. I clambered out of the backseat of Jude's truck, suddenly remembering Liam's hint that there was a surprise waiting for me here. God, I hoped it wasn't a party. There were no cars around, the lights were off, and we'd just left everybody at Sunday dinner, but I still wondered what was up. Maybe there would be cake in there somewhere. Then I'd at least have something to eat for breakfast. Damn, I sucked at adulting. I should have had them stop at the grocery store.

I pulled the key Liam had given me from my pocket along with the paper with the alarm code. Ready or not, I was about to become a real grownup. No more running from place to place, no more flitting from idea to idea, and no more jumping into things headfirst.

"Well, here goes nothing," I muttered.

"You got this, Holly. I shouldn't have said anything in the truck." Levi pulled me in for a side hug.

"No, it's okay. I appreciate it. I think I'll be okay but I'm glad to know I have a place to go, you know?"

"We're cool then?"

"Always." I unlocked the door; Jude flicked the lights on as I entered the alarm code.

"That door is good," he murmured as he stepped inside. "Solid."

It was clean with a fresh coat of paint covering most of the walls. The gross shag carpet had been removed. "It looks nice." The area where Luke and Liam had removed the wall was where the sales counter would be set up. More work would be needed back there, and I was excited to go over the plans with Luke and Gram.

"Let's get these boxes upstairs." Jude suggested.

I followed them up the two flights, then the spiral staircase leading to what would be my cozy little escape from the world.

I stopped dead in my tracks at the top stair. "You guys . . ." I breathed. "What did you do?"

"We all chipped in," Levi answered. "We couldn't let you live out of boxes and use a sleeping bag on the floor, Holly." He scoffed and put his hand over his heart . "What kind of siblings do you think we are?"

Tears filled my eyes.

The fucking best, that's what they were.

I spun in a circle taking it all in. There was a bed and a side table, just like I'd envisioned in the turret room. The big bed was covered with one of Gram's quilts. I let out a sob when I flicked the light on to find a few of her paintings hanging on the wall and curtains that I knew my mother had sewn long ago covering the windows. "You guys . . ." I repeated.

"Take a look over here." Jude had set my box down in one of the bedrooms. I peeked inside to find a dresser, a bookshelf filled with books, and a chair for reading.

"Jude . . ." I breathed.

Levi led me to the small living area. "This is all new. Violet picked it out, obviously, since most of it is purple." The tiny living room was now fully furnished. A couch, cozy chair, pillows, throw blankets, tables, plants, family photos, and cute decorations filled the room. They had thought of everything, and even better, they knew what I would like. Levi beamed at me as he said, "We got you the TV." Of course they did. It was huge.

"We got your internet hooked up too," Jude said. "The WiFi password is Bilbo69Baggins, with both Bs capitalized."

"Thank you!" Sobbing, I held my arms out, and I laughed through my tears when they enveloped me in a huge hug. "I love you guys."

"We love you too," Jude said as he gave me an extra squeeze. "And listen, this was almost a big-ass surprise party, but we knew you'd hate everything about that. Except for cake. And yes, there is one. It's chocolate, and it's in the fridge downstairs. Mom made it. So, you're welcome."

"You'll be all set for morning." Levi ruffled my hair. "There's food in the kitchen, too. Mom and Rose went shopping and stocked the fridge and cupboards for you. Violet bought you a coffee maker but told us to let you know she'll open the shop and you can come in for coffee with her whenever you're ready."

"I can't believe you guys did all this for me."

"We missed you, Holls. And all of us want you to stay in Sweetbriar."

"I love it. I love all of you. I'm going to learn how to cook and make a big dinner to say thank you."

"Meatloaf," Levi declared. "Have mom teach you to make it. I'll come over and learn with you. We can figure out the mashed potatoes ourselves. It can't be that hard, right?"

"Right? I mean, boil them, mash them . . ."

He threw his hands out wide. "Exactly."

"Like, now that I have my own kitchen, I'm motivated to cook. What's that about?"

"Maybe because you want to bake Liam some snickerdoodles?" Jude teased. *Had everyone heard about that?* Cinnamon was his thing and I wanted—damn it—I just wanted to make him smile. Maybe there was a snickerdoodle holiday I could use as an excuse.

"Hmm, maybe." I was so happy, I laughed instead of slugging him in the arm for teasing me.

"One more thing before we go." Levi stepped back and aimed his phone at me. "Smile. It's for the group text."

I curved my lips into a quivering smile with tears streaming down my face. "This picture is going to be horrible."

He grinned at me and said, "It's perfect. Don't wipe your nose."

"Levi!" I squealed when I realized how bad it was running. "Take another one."

"Nope." He pocketed his phone. "That shot captured everything," he teased.

"I don't like leaving you here without a car," Jude muttered.

"Well, I can't afford one yet and Lily's is back at her house. I can't keep borrowing it."

He raised an eyebrow at me. "Did she say that?"

"Well, no. She offered to give it to me, in fact."

"We'll bring it over tomorrow. Don't be a dumbass. You can't walk everywhere. What if it rains? And this is Sweetbriar—it could hail or snow at any given minute no matter what season it is. You know that."

"You're probably right," I conceded. "But I'm not letting her give it to me."

"Whatever, as long as you have transportation. And I don't mean an umbrella and a bicycle, okay?"

"Fine. I agree."

"Okay, we'll get going and leave you to it."

I followed them downstairs, with only a slight sense of trepidation about being alone in this massive old house.

No, I'd be okay.

I got this.

And who would know if I ran back upstairs and turned all the lights on behind myself? No one, that's who. I was the boss and if I wanted a massive electric bill, no one could stop me. So ha!

I used to sleep all by myself in a tent *outside*, for eff's sake. I could sleep in a house with four walls, steel doors, and a state-of-the-art alarm system. Dang it.

Suddenly my phone blew up with text messages.

Startled, I let out a scream and almost fell over my own feet as I fumbled with my phone to see who it was.

It was every single one of my siblings plus Mom, Dad, and Gram offering to come over and spend the night with me.

Laughing, I locked up behind my brothers and armed the alarm, watching through the window as they drove away. Once their truck had cleared the end of the street, the silence of the house echoed in my ears and yeah, I hauled ass up the stairs, flicking on every last light as I went.

I decided there was no shame in that. It was my first night here totally alone in this huge, old house that totally was *not* haunted. *Damn it, Lily.* I'd cut down on my night light need gradually but for now, it was going to be just like daylight up in here.

I made it to the turret and slid a curtain aside so I could peer down at the street. It was deserted. The railroad tracks were across the road, and I remembered how the sound of the trains used to freak me out when I was a little kid spending the night here with Gram and Grandpa. Anything could be on the trains, from anywhere. I shivered and shoved the curtain back in place.

Wait.

I moved it aside again, just enough to peek through. Someone was jogging up the street. I squinted, waiting for him to pass beneath the streetlight.

It was Liam.

I watched as he stopped and raised a hand to his forehead, as if gazing in my direction, to look at the house.

Was he checking up on me?

Who cared? I didn't have to be alone here. I dashed down the stairs and made it to the front door just as he was about to ring the bell.

I threw the door open, beaming at his questioning face.

"Are you okay?" he asked.

"What are you doing here?" I realized my words did not match my actions when I grabbed him by the hands and pulled him inside, slamming the door behind his body and rearming the alarm. "I mean, welcome to my home. I have cake."

"I couldn't sleep so I went out for a jog. I could see the house from all the way up the road. It's lit up so bright I wondered if the place was on fire."

"Uhh, yeah. I guess I got a little nervous . . ."

The back of his hand drifted softly down my cheek before he caught himself, drawing back like I was the one on fire and not the house like he had thought. "Hey, there's nothing wrong with that. This place is huge, anyone would be nervous their first night alone here. And did you say cake? It's almost Make Up Your Own Holiday Day and I could go for a slice of cake."

"Wow, Make Up Your Own Holiday Day? Forget the freakin' cake. We could do literally anything we wanted to." The reality of what I'd said out loud hit me as the idea of doing whatever I wanted with him sent my body into overdrive imagining all the things we could do. Now I felt lucky to have this huge place all to myself.

His eyes turned lazy as they drifted first to my mouth, then back up to meet my gaze again. "Yeah, we can, starting at midnight."

"Maybe you could kiss me again for a little bit." Being this close to him with none of my self-imposed rules to get in the way was a heady feeling. But then, my feelings for him had nothing to do with reason.

He towered over me, shoulders bowed forward, hands sliding around my waist as he backed me toward the staircase. "We could get it out of our system again until we're ready for more."

I held onto his forearms for balance. "God, yes. What time is it?"

He pulled one hand away just long enough for his eyes to dart to his watch then back to mine. "We have a little less than fifteen minutes to decide."

"I've already decided, and the answer is yes." I let go and turned to pace a circle around the room like a caged animal, contemplating the inevitable choice I had made.

Something about those holidays he kept coming up with had emboldened me. I knew it didn't really take away the consequences of my actions, but I decided to use it as an excuse anyway.

"Hey, we don't have to do anything. We could always eat cake and talk. Or I could go back home."

I spun to face him. "No. Don't leave. Please?"

"I'm here. I'm not going anywhere Holly." His smile was soft, comforting. It belied the fire in his eyes and the intensity that burned in the deep gravel of his voice. "Lately there's no other place I'd rather be than where you are. Don't you know that by now?"

"I know it. I feel it too."

"Good, then get back over here. We have about ten minutes left to be sure."

"Come upstairs with me? I have an actual living room up there. We could get comfortable."

He grinned. "I know you do."

I remembered his earlier mention of a surprise. "Ahhh, of course you know. You probably helped them set it up, didn't you?"

"I did."

"I'm so lucky to have so many awesome people in my life. My family, friends, now you. Especially you. I was so scared that maybe I was dead inside. But whenever I'm with you Liam, you make me feel hopeful and I don't want to lose that." I heard the words I'd just said and cringed internally. "Ohhh, crap, please shut me up. I'm saying too much. Way, way too much. We're not even dating each other right now. We're just friends . . ."

"No, it's not too much, not at all. I get it." He reached out, brushing his hand down my cheek in an almost wistful gesture. I wanted to lean into his touch, but he drew his hand away before I could. "I had forgotten who I was before I enlisted. I have flashes of that life, but I can't feel it anymore. Then I got out and couldn't seem to figure out how to just *be* anymore. Be still. Be present. Just be in a room and relax inside of a moment. But whenever I'm with you, I feel everything. You make me feel like myself again."

Tears filled my eyes as I thrilled to his words, to the fact that I could do such a thing for him. "I love that."

His hand slid down my arm to grasp mine, strong, firm, protective. "I do too."

"I'm not going to mess this up, Liam. I'll never forgive myself if I do." I was giving him everything I had and yet keeping a few things to myself at the same time. But somehow it was okay. With him I could be honest about my emotions but keep a guard on my heart. He radiated patience and kindness, and I couldn't seem to get enough of him.

"I won't either. I won't let us."

"Promise?"

He lifted my hand to kiss the inside of my wrist, eyes locked to mine as his lips lingered against my skin. "I promise you, sunshine. You'll always be safe with me." The soft brush of his lips sent me spiraling as the desire to feel more of him overrode everything else.

I let my eyes drift closed, shutting them tight as I tried to hide the overwhelming intensity of my reaction to being this close to him. I squeezed his hand in mine and reached out blindly with the other. As soon as my fingers slid against the solid warmth of his palm I relaxed. Even though he had sent me flying, he also anchored me, and I knew I would be okay.

"I got you," he whispered, lifting my hands to his lips. And I believed him. He had me, but I had him too. There was no rush, and for the first time in my life I knew I had no reason to be afraid of how I felt. I just needed to be ready for it.

"I'm okay," I breathed. "This is fine, we'll be fine."

"It's midnight, sunshine."

I opened my eyes as an anticipatory shudder shot through my body. "So, kiss me."

Chapter 12
Liam

That first kiss we shared on Valentine's Day had snuck up on me, carrying me away to the point I could barely remember it. It felt so much like a dream, almost like it wasn't real.

And here we were again, on a random holiday I'd found online, about to do it again. But this time we knew what we were getting into. I hadn't planned to see her tonight. I couldn't sleep; that wasn't a lie. But maybe I should have planned this. If I had, I'd have been better prepared to handle the rush of feelings that were now flooding my system.

She was so fucking pretty with her pink cheeks, upturned lips, and all that gorgeous long blonde hair. I'd spent so many nights fantasizing about wrapping my hands in it again, touching her, feeling her against me, and now it was about to happen again. Finally.

She wasn't the only one afraid of being dead inside. I had been living in the dark, but she made me feel things

I'd never felt before in my life. She lit me up, she made me burn. I was playing with fire tonight and could end up getting hurt, but it didn't matter. I'd do anything to get another taste of her.

But I had to maintain control of the situation; I couldn't push too hard. I had the feeling if we went too far tonight it would destroy everything. Any chance I had with her would vanish and to lose her before having a real shot at having her would be terrible. I knew without a doubt I wanted her in my life, and in this moment I could no longer ignore what I'd been too scared to admit to myself.

She was the one.

Since I first saw her, it was *her*. I felt the possibility of it then, but I sure as fuck knew it now. I'd been starved for someone like her, someone who could understand me and what I'd been through. Not only understand it, but want to help me through it. Her compassion and empathy were irresistible, her beautiful face and body were beyond temptation. *She was mine.* And I would do anything for her—including keeping distance between us right now, if that's what she needed.

I pulled reluctantly back, holding her at arms' length.

Her eyebrows pinched together in confusion. "Liam . . .?"

"We don't have to do anything. We both know holiday hall passes aren't a real thing, we both know we're not quite ready to get serious, and it's okay if you change your mind. Are you sure you want to do this?"

She stepped close, her soft hands sliding up my chest as a look of certainty flashed in her eyes. "I am if you are."

"Oh, I'm sure. You have no idea what you do to me, do you?" Her nearness was as much comfort as it was torture, but nothing would tear me away as long as she wanted me to be here.

"Probably the same thing you do to me." Her voice faded out into the air between us, but I heard every word.

"Upstairs?"

She nodded. "Let's go. A kiss against the wall again would be hot, but I'd rather get cozy with you."

Without a word, I swept her into my arms and started up the stairs. Cozy sounded amazing and I didn't want to wait. Midnight had passed; we were running out of time.

"Liam! You can't carry me up two flights of stairs and a spiral staircase!"

He laughed. "I can't?"

"I'll rephrase. I believe you absolutely can, and while this demonstration of your astounding musculature has me feeling all feminine and girly and might actually make me *squee* out loud, you don't have to do this. I can walk."

"Tonight will end, sunshine, along with our excuses, and I want you as close as I can get you while it lasts."

"*Squeeeee*," she murmured with a grin as she looped her arms around my neck. "How are you so amazing?"

"It's all you. You bring it out in me."

"Oh my god . . ." She tucked her head against my chest, and I huffed out a gentle laugh as her body went limp and she relaxed into my arms.

I stopped briefly on the second set of stairs to drop a kiss to the top of her head. I thought about how she fit into my arms right now and how she'd fit herself right into my heart like she belonged there from the second we'd met.

I met her while lost in a cloud of grief and doubts and little by little she'd become an essential part of my life. She was one of those things that was perfect as they were—the perfect friend who gave me the exact comfort and care and fun I needed.

Did I really want to risk this?

She was becoming one of the most important friendships of my life.

Why should she be saddled with someone as damaged as me?

I couldn't even fucking sleep for fuck's sake. I doubted more than I was sure of, and I knew in my bones she deserved better.

"I can hear you thinking. Quit it."

"What?"

"You're wound tight tonight, Liam. I can tell. The gears in your head are spinning out of control."

"Oh yeah? Maybe I need somebody to unwind me."

"I'm good at that. March that hot ass of yours upstairs and kiss me. Whatever is bothering you, forget about it."

She knew me so well. "What if I can't?"

"I have shit I can't let go of too. But tonight is not about that. Tonight has somehow become about me and you shoving everything bad to the side and letting ourselves feel good for a change. We can think about it tomorrow. Fuck the consequences."

"Fuck the consequences," I repeated.

"Yeah," she whispered. "Okay?"

I hoisted her higher and jogged the rest of the way up the stairs. The spiral staircase was too narrow to carry her up, so I set her down and backed her toward the sectional couch in the corner. It was my housewarming gift to her and I'd placed at an angle near the gas brick fireplace this morning. I snatched up the remote control I'd left on the mantel and started a fire.

She sat down with a bemused smile. "I didn't even notice this when I got here. I'm so lucky."

"I bought it for you. You're welcome." I nudged her backward on the chaise end and dug my knee into the cushion between hers as I pushed up over her. "Is this still okay?" I all but growled as the leash I kept strung up tight on myself slowly unraveled.

"Yes." She reached up, hands around my neck, to pull me the rest of the way down.

Our lips met as we crashed together in a tangle of limbs, mouths opening to each other, hands everywhere. We'd gone from zero to sixty in one hot second and I couldn't get enough. I feared I would never get enough when it came to her.

The kiss lingered even as I pulled back to shift her to the side as not to crush her with my weight. I could still taste her, sweet as honey on my lips, as she smiled up at me.

"I don't want to take more than you want to give," I whispered. "Do you think this is a mistake?"

"No, I don't."

"I don't either." I shifted higher on the cushions as she hitched her leg over my thigh with that pretty yellow sundress she'd had on at dinner riding high on her hips.

Once again, nothing but a thin pair of panties separated my body and her soft warm heat. And my leash was now threadbare.

It took all my willpower not to unzip my jeans, shove those panties to the side and sink into her. I wanted her so goddamned bad.

She was made for me. We both knew it. It was in every interaction we'd ever shared; it wrapped around us like a warm blanket; it made us safe, keeping us close even though we were both full of fears and doubts that could drive us apart if we weren't careful.

I reclaimed her lips, crushing her against my chest as I kissed her breathless and moved my hand up her silky thigh to skim over her perfect round ass and pull her closer, keeping her still as I pressed myself hard against her.

"You feel so good. God, how I want you, Liam . . ."

"I want you too. Way too much for tonight."

She fell against the back of the couch and propped her head on her hand with a scowl. "I don't have any condoms here, damn it. We should probably stop. Or at least reframe our expectations before we continue."

Her legs twined through mine as her arm snaked around my waist. I hauled her close as the inferno we'd built between us settled into something manageable, something we could contain.

I hesitated a moment before speaking, watching her in profile as she let out a soft sigh.

"I haven't even taken you on a proper date yet. We can't talk about condoms until I at least pick you up, open a few doors, hold your hand, and share a meal with you. My grandma would come back and haunt me into oblivion if we had sex tonight anyway."

She dropped her chin on my chest with a quiet laugh. "Shh, don't talk about ghosts in here, I'm pretty sure this place is actually haunted. And hey, you fixed me breakfast after my dramatic traipse through the woods and took me shopping with you for Cheddar. That's high-quality date stuff as far as I'm concerned. Oh! And don't forget the waffle tacos and *Lord of the Rings*."

I leaned forward to press my forehead to hers. "You know what I mean."

Her eyes sparkled this close. "You're old-fashioned. I kind of like it."

"Well, I believe in respect, manners, and protecting the woman I'm with. If that's old-fashioned, I'll take it."

"I'll take it too." She dropped a kiss to my throat for emphasis. "Bag it up, I'm sold."

"How are you so fucking cute?"

"Most people would not call it that, but thanks. Make out with me? If we're lucky we can get each other off on it."

I burst out laughing. "Your smart mouth is amazing."

Her hands crept down over my ass, giving it a

squeeze. "Wait 'til you see what it can do when you're naked."

"I could tell you the same thing."

"I'm making a mental list, Liam, just so you know."

"I'll check all your boxes, sunshine. Count on it. Don't I get a nickname too?"

She pursed her lips, putting on a show of thinking about it. "I like the way Liam sounds. And I think I'll like it even more if you can make me scream it."

I buried my face in her neck, licking up the delicate column of her throat. "You're a bad girl, aren't you?" I whispered into her ear before nipping at the lobe.

She froze in my arms. "So they say . . ."

"Oh god, oh shit. Holly, sweetheart, I'm so sorry." I tried to meet her eyes, but they were glued somewhere in the vicinity of my chest. "To be clear, I don't know what *they* say, and I don't want to know. I was flirting, poorly, obviously, since you've referred to your reputation before and I should have remembered that. I think you're sexy as hell, hilarious, and more beautiful than any woman I've ever seen in my life. I didn't mean anything by—"

Sighing, she put a delicate fingertip to my lips. "I know you didn't and I'm sorry about how I reacted. I just, um . . . shit. I need to get over it." She flopped back and ran a hand into her hair. "I need to forget about it. Who cares what people I don't even like think about me? Right? I ruined the mood, didn't I?"

"Not at all." I took her hand and kissed the back of it before cradling her face in my palms. "What do we have if we're not honest with each other?"

Blinking rapidly, she smiled. "I don't know. I've never had anything like this before."

I smiled in response before continuing. "I haven't either, but I know what I want to have, and that's everything I've found so far with you."

"I want it too. So much, you have no idea."

"Then come here." I pulled her head to my chest and wrapped her up in my arms. I needed to hold her, to be close. She needed comfort and so did I.

"What are we doing?" she murmured.

I shrugged. "Acting like responsible adults who know what they're not ready for?"

"I think you're onto something." Her arms tightened around me. "Are we communicating effectively?"

I barked out a laugh. "We sure as hell are. I think we're setting healthy boundaries too."

We held each other quietly, settling into each other's arms as we let the pressure of the moment fade away.

"Want to watch *The Return of the King* and do first base stuff in my new living room upstairs?" she finally said, breaking the companiable silence we'd sunken into. "I have a purple couch and a huge TV."

"I would love that."

She sat up and I smirked as her eyes snapped to the television I'd installed this morning above her fireplace. "Hey." She giggled and turned to face me. "Did you put that there?"

"Yeah, and I admit I may have had ulterior motives with this couch-fireplace-TV combo."

"Would you look at that? Suddenly I have two TV's

and a friend with possibilities. You're a freaking sweetheart. Thank you, Liam." She cupped my chin in her palm and smacked a quick kiss to my lips. "And you also have a standing invitation. Movie night at Holly's haunted house. Plan on it."

"I'll bring the popcorn."

She beamed at me. "I'm learning to cook meatloaf and snickerdoodles. I'll make dinner."

"My favorites." I tried to find more words. But they were gone, lost in this perfect night. Sometime in between her throwing the door open and right now, something had shifted between us. If words had any real meaning in this world, hers had the power to fill me up where I hadn't even realized I was empty.

So we cuddled under one of my grandmother's knitted blankets I had placed on the back of the couch and watched the movie. Occasionally we would kiss or hug each other tighter, and it was all we needed. Later on we'd need more, but for now, this was perfect.

Chapter 13
Holly

At dawn, Liam had tucked me into my brand-new bed and kissed me goodbye. He told me to sleep for a few hours while he went home to shower and get ready to come back here for work. Lucky me that I would have him around all day.

Sunlight streamed through my turret windows just the way I remembered it from when I was a kid, and I smiled. How had I managed to get so fortunate?

My phone pinged with a few incoming texts, and I fumbled for it on my bedside table.

It was Gram. And Liam.

LIAM: Good morning, sunshine.

My heart turned over in my chest. We weren't officially dating, and we deliberately did *not* have sex last night and he still sent me a good morning text. *Amazing.*

ME: I can't wait to see you.

LIAM: It's mutual. Be there soon.

GRAM: Sugar pie, I'm coming over with coffee and breakfast from Vi's. Time to rise and shine and make plans!

ME: I'm up and can't wait! See you later.

I quickly changed into a pair of shorts and a hoodie then dashed down the stairs to meet Gram.

She was already ringing the doorbell when I finally made it to the ground floor.

"I'm coming!"

I threw open the door to find Owen on the other side, wearing a tool-belt and clearly ready to work. "Well, isn't this a surprise. Been a long time, Holly. You still look good." His eyes ran up and down my body almost too fast for me to realize he'd done it, but not quite.

"Yeah, um, hi…"

He pushed his way around me, headed for the area in

the rear of the room where Liam and Luke had torn the wall down. "I'm supposed to finish work on the wood floor," he stated.

"All right. I guess that's fine. I'll leave you to it." For lack of anything better to do, I headed into the kitchen to wait for Gram and check out what Rose and my mother had bought.

Footsteps across the floor made me turn around. Insistent hands at my hips made me see red.

"Babe, I saw how you checked me out and the answer is yes. Remember how hot we used to be together?" Owen dug his fingers into the sides of my ass, leering at my mouth as he tried to pull me into his body for a kiss.

"What the hell, Owen?" I twisted away, taking a few steps back. "Get out of here."

"You don't have to fight it. I won't say a word." He reached out, catching the back of my neck with his palm.

"What are you doing? Let go of me!" He didn't let go; he yanked me closer. He had never been rough with me like this before. It was shocking and scary. "You're hurting me."

"Stop fighting me, Holly. We both know what you need—"

"Yoo hoo! Door is open, Holly, honey. It's Gram!"

Owen went still and I took the opportunity to step back then punch him in the stomach, stomp on his foot, and give him a good shove. I was fists up and ready for more when he started yelling.

"What the fuck, Holly? You bitch!"

"Just what in the hell is going on here?" Gram entered the kitchen. "Watch your mouth, Owen."

"Nothing is going on," he wheezed, hands to his stomach. "Just a misunderstanding is all—"

"Get the hell out of here, Owen," I ground out. "Get out before I finish you off, and I do not mean the way you intended when you grabbed my ass." I held onto my temper by a thread. One more word out of his stupid mouth and I'd let it go.

"I see, I get it. Not all men, right? But somehow, it's always a damn man," Gram tutted. "It's time for you to go, Owen." She pulled her cell out of her handbag. "I'm calling Luke."

Owen knocked the phone out of her hand, and it skittered across the floor. "I'll go. Let's leave Luke out of this. I need this job. I got kids."

Enraged, I growled, "Don't you dare touch her," shoving him hard with my hands to his shoulders.

He stumbled backward a step but this time he shoved me back. I went flying into the wall. "Bitch, I said don't touch me again." I couldn't wrap my head around how he was acting. This was not how I remembered him. Not one bit.

"Oh, but I thought you wanted me to touch you." I sauntered toward him, ready to unleash the full force of my fury. "Is this not quite what you had in mind?"

Gram darted toward the phone mounted near the wide arched entry to the kitchen.

"What the hell is going on here?!" It was Liam and

his voice was like a thunderbolt, literally echoing around the empty foyer.

I froze, eyes darting to where Liam stood, staring Owen down like he was about to kill him.

"Oh, you're screwed now, sonny." Gram laughed. "He called Holly a bitch and shoved her damn near across the room. And just so you know, Owen, I never liked you."

Liam's voice dropped even lower and he went completely still. "You're fired. Leave. And you better make it fast before I end you right now."

"You can't fire me! She attacked me! She's fucking crazy, man." Owen stepped up to Liam. "Luke wants the floor finished, he said—"

"Do you really want to find out what Luke has to *say* after I tell him you put your hands on his sister-in-law?"

Owen blanched and shook his head.

"I didn't think so."

"You know what? Fuck this. I'm not losing my job over a demented slut like her. She knows I work for Luke, and she knew I was coming by. She fucking wanted it and all I did was try to give it to her. We almost got married so I know how hot she can get—"

Liam's growl shut him up fast and I swear I could see Owen's throat muscles work as he gulped.

Liam finally moved, stalking across the floor to where Owen stood. "Keep talking, I dare you."

"Look at her." He flung out a hand in my direction. "Everyone in town knows what she's like, man. Wearing those tight little shorts and looking at me the way that she did. She practically begged me to fuck her. Everyone knows what a whore she became after me. You've probably had a piece of her too. Is she still good? I'd really like to know."

Gram stepped forward, cutting off Liam's advance. "I should have stuck you with a knitting needle instead of trying to call Luke, you little shit," Gram snarled. "Restraint gets you nowhere, Holly. Remember that, and don't ever feel bad for sticking up for yourself."

He turned on Gram. "You probably want it too, you batty old bitch."

Liam's voice roared, "That's it! I've heard enough." He picked Owen up by his upper arms as if he were a toddler and walked him to the open front door where he proceeded to toss him through it like a sack of trash into a dumpster. Owen stumbled backward over his feet a few steps before landing in the hedges that lined the front lawn. "Don't come back here. Do not think of coming anywhere near Holly, or this house, or Rosemary, or any of the Barretts ever again. And if one more word about her ever comes out of your filthy fucking mouth you won't be dealing with Luke or the police, you'll deal with me. Do you get what that means?"

"Yeah, I get you, man. Chill. I'll go. Don't call the fucking cops."

"Aw, too late." Gram laughed. "I already did."

Liam was still glaring at Owen when he gestured in our direction. "Apologize to them. Now."

"Sorry," Owen shouted weakly.

"Do not accept it," he turned to instruct me and

Gram. "He doesn't exist for you." He turned back to Owen. "And if you don't do what I said, if you think about coming back here to mess things up, or make threats, you won't exist for *anyone*."

I stood there blinking in shock while Gram let out another satisfied laugh.

No man had ever defended my honor like that. My heart pounded so hard I could feel it in my ears.

We watched Owen get into his truck and drive away.

"He just threw him," Gram announced as if I hadn't just seen him do it. "Picked him up and tossed his stupid little ass right out the door." She turned toward our personal hero. "I knew I liked you, Liam. I was right about you. You're a good man."

Liam slammed the door and grunted in response.

"He's a good man, Holly."

"Yeah, I know he is." I knew it before, but if I'd had any doubt about it, today would have blasted that doubt into smithereens because, *damn*.

Liam grunted again and ran his hands into his hair. I could tell he was trying to calm down before he said anything else. Every muscle in his body was strung tight and I watched his jaw tick as he ground his teeth together. I wanted to help him calm down, but I had no idea how when I was about to freak right the fuck out. Plus, I was still skating on the edge of my own temper. I was halfway tempted to march over to Owen's house and finish kicking his ass. What the hell had gotten into him?

"Let's all settle down and go sit at the table." Gram suggested. "I called Cade and your daddy so they can take care of Owen." My older brother, Cade was a Sweet-briar cop, and my dad was the chief. "Now we can call Luke, and you can tell him you told him so, Liam. There's a certain satisfaction in being right about something, even if the proof is a pile of shit. That's just the way it is, am I right?" Gram and her unique sense of logic to the rescue.

Liam cracked half a smile.

"Gram, I freaking love you." I was so glad I had her in my life.

"Well, I love you too, honey and you're going to be okay. I promise you, you will be okay."

Tears filled my eyes, but I blinked them away before they had a chance to fall. "I know. I always am."

"I shouldn't have let him go," Liam finally stated. "I should have beat the shit out of him. I'm sorry."

"Uh, do not apologize. What you did was perfectly fine with me. In fact, it was better than beating him up. Like, how embarrassing, right? He's a grown man and you picked him up like a little kid." I covered my mouth as a hysterical laugh burst out.

Suddenly Liam was right in front of me, hands cupping my face as he stared intently into my eyes. "He's full of shit."

I shrugged and looked away. "Yeah, I know."

He lowered his head so his gaze was level with mine. "Holly, look at me. What he said is bullshit. Utter garbage. Do not take it in, do you hear me?"

Still shaken from what happened, I looked at him. "I hear you, Liam. I promise I do."

"Good. I'm sorry, but I have to go. I have to cool off

before I find him and finish this how I should have before. I have to talk to Luke. I will lock up behind myself. Do not open that door for anyone. I'll pick up a temporary security camera and install it tonight. The shop's cameras are on backorder. I shouldn't have waited for them. I'm sorry."

"Stop apologizing to me. None of this is your fault. I'm not your responsibility. I'm a grownup. Cade will take care of Owen and it will be fine. My dad will probably insist on sleeping here for at least a week," I joked. "Plus, I can take care of myself. I've been doing it for years." I knew my smile was shaky, but I had to reassure him.

He stepped closer. "No, you don't take care of yourself when shit like this happens. Not anymore. From now on it's me you come to when you need anything. I'm the man you run to. Not your father, not your brothers. *Me.* Do you understand?"

"Oh snap," Gram said under her breath.

"I understand," I whispered.

"Good." He traced a fingertip down my cheek, ending beneath my chin to tip it up before placing a gentle kiss on my lips. "Have breakfast with your grandma, sunshine. I'll be back soon."

"Okay . . ." I breathed out.

Gram and I watched as he quickly strode to the door. We heard the locks turn into place and the beeps beep into—whatever, as he set the alarm.

"What just happened?" I asked.

"That was the sound of your man telling it like it is, honey."

"*Pffft* . . ." I deflated, knees bending until I was sitting crisscross on the floor with my head in my hands. This was too much. The day had barely started, and I was already in over my head. What in the hell had gotten into Owen? He had to be on drugs or something.

"Listen to me, Holly. You don't find the man of your dreams, he finds you. And he'll wait if he has to."

"Holy shit," I mumbled into my hands.

"Damn straight. You got yourself a good one, too. I've had my eye on him since he started coming around with Luke. Lily just adores him, the kids do too. He's a good man. I knew it—just like your grandpa, that one is. Sweet to the core. Good men wait for what they want because they always know what they need."

"Well, *I* need coffee." I stood.

Gram patted my back. "Go to the table, sugar pie. I'll get you fixed up."

"I'm so glad you're here. I didn't want to have to—"

"Oh goodness, my sweet girl. I know." She pulled me into her arms and stroked my back. "I know, baby, I know, *shh*."

"I don't want to cry about this anymore."

"Crying is good for you. Let it out, I won't judge you." She pulled back and slipped a hankie into my hand. "Go on to the table and get started on breakfast. I'm going to make a call. Well, if I can find my blasted phone, that is."

I spotted it on the floor and retrieved it for her before heading into the kitchen.

Gram joined me a few minutes later.

"I called your mama."

"Gram! You know we haven't been getting along—"

"Hush. I've had enough of that. She's on her way. This is the perfect time for the two of you to make up. You need her right now."

"Great, fine, whatever," I muttered, too tired and messed up over what had happened to argue. And Gram was right, I did need her.

"It's time to nip all this vitriol between you two in the bud. Listen to your grandma. It's all a bunch of silly misunderstandings because the two of you are too stubborn to talk it out and you both know it."

I sipped my coffee then shoved half a chocolate muffin in my mouth with a half-hearted glare aimed her way. She was right, I should talk to my mom. But now? Hadn't I been through enough today?

We could see the front yard from the breakfast nook in the kitchen. Gram pulled the curtains aside so we could watch for my mother. Unfortunately, Jared pulled up first. When it rained, did it have to freakin' pour too? Dang.

Gram *tsked*. "I didn't invite that little turd, Holly. Dammit."

"I know you didn't." Gram knew how I felt about Jared. She was a big proponent of not humoring people for the sake of being nice. She was the only one who seemed to realize what a pesty little shit he'd been toward me for almost my entire life. "Just tell him to fuck right off if he gives you any lip."

"You know why I don't," I hissed under my breath.

"His ding-bat mother is friends with your mama, yeah, yeah, yeah, I know. She's a sweetheart, but she raised a useless turd of a son."

Jared headed up the walkway, with a wave and a grin.

"Could this day get any worse, Gram? I don't think so," I whined in a sing-song voice.

"We don't have to let him in. Liam said not to."

"He saw us through the window. Plus, he approves the building permits for Sweetbriar. Did you know that?"

"So he has to approve our store plans?"

I heaved out a sigh. "Yep. Come on." We headed to the foyer to let him in.

"Ladies," he greeted. "I hope you're doing well," he addressed Gram.

"Just fine. What can we do for you?"

"I'm here about your permits, and to remind Holly about the festival."

I let my eyes drift toward the window with a heavy sigh. I had lost the will to put up a front for him. "I haven't forgotten."

"Good. It's next weekend. I'll pick you up in the morning and help you get set up, then introduce you around."

"I don't know if her boyfriend will like that," Gram muttered as she aimed a mischievous look at me behind Jared's back.

My eyes bugged out. "Gram!" I thought about the

permits and her dream of reopening this place. "He's not my boyfriend."

"Who's not your boyfriend? Liam? Luke's Army friend? The one you were with at Tess's store the other day?" He slung questions at me rapid fire, like arrows.

"I don't have a boyfriend. Gram is just trying her hand at matchmaking, like Violet. Right, Gram?"

She shrugged.

"Are you dating him?"

"No. Like I told you before, I'm not ready to jump back into the dating world yet."

"Oh, but sweetie, this won't be a date." He sifted his fingers through the ends of my hair, and I wanted to slug him like I'd just done to Owen, but I restrained myself and instead took a step back. "This is business, remember?"

Think of the permits. Think of Gram. Think of my future adorable and awesome apothecary store and do not punch him in his fucking face. I dug my fingernails into my hand as I tried to keep my rapidly unraveling temper in check.

"Ahh, strictly business. I see." Gram had always been suspicious of him, and it made me feel validated. Everyone in town adored Jared, even my own family. I'd always felt kind of bad that I didn't. "Then you won't mind if I tag along with you? This is my shop too, after all."

Jared paused, visibly struggling with what to say. His weak smile didn't reach his eyes, and his response was half-hearted. "Of course I don't mind. I'll pick you ladies up the morning of. Around 8?" He handed me a manila envelope. "Have Luke look these over."

"Sounds good. Thanks for thinking of us, Jared."

He passed my mother on the walkway as he left. "Mrs. Barrett." He nodded to her then got into his car.

"I didn't realize you two were the hanging-out-together type of friends," she observed as she entered. Gram locked the door and reprogrammed the alarm behind her.

"We're not."

"Of course they're not. You know that, Dahlia."

"Ugh, Mother, I can't stand him. Don't you realize that by now? I'm sorry you're friends with his mother but I can't pretend anymore. It's time to stop trying to fix me up with him."

Her look of affront surprised me. "I haven't tried to fix you up with Jared in years. And darling, you look harried. What are you upset about?"

"Harried? Okay. You know what? Don't worry about it."

"Now hold on a minute. I'm your mother. I can worry about all kinds of things at the same time. We'll get to the bottom of the Jared thing. And I'll help you with whatever is troubling you—"

"I'm fine. Leave me to my drama so I can burn it out in peace. I'm about to lose my temper and I don't want to take it out on you, so please don't push me."

"Hush, both of you," Gram started. "I didn't call you over here to argue, Dahlia."

Mom's eyes got big. "Wait a second, is that it?"

"What are you talking about?" I asked. "Just spit it out. Is *what* it?"

Her face fell. "Oh god. That's it. I'm the problem. I'm so sorry."

"What, why are you sorry?" I was stunned. "What are you talking about? Jared?"

"No, not Jared. *Me.* I won't push to try to help you anymore, Holly." Her expression softened. "I'll let you burn it out, like you just said. I'll only offer help if you ask for it."

Gram's head darted between us, back and forth, like she was watching a tennis game. "What's happening? I swear, I will never understand the two of you."

I stared at my mother as she finally understood what had been our problem for years, which was her butting into my business, me getting angry, then the both of us ignoring the issue until somehow it blew over. Rinse and repeat for my entire life. This didn't happen with her and my other siblings.

"I think we'll get along from now on. I'll make everything better. No more meddling, no more trying to fix things for you. I will just listen to you quietly from now on, Holly. Would you like a hug?"

My jaw dropped. "I mean, I guess I could use a hug."

"Forget about these muffins." She pulled me into her arms. "How about we go for a burger at Holloway's?" she whispered in my ear. "It's still early, but I have a craving."

"I could eat a burger," I whispered back. "Can we have milkshakes too?"

"Of course we can. My treat, darling."

"What's happening here?" Gram was confused and I didn't blame her. My mother and I could make up and keep an argument going at the same time. We were weird that way. But it seemed like those days might be over. If she stuck to her no-meddling declaration, that was.

I pulled away, feeling a bit better. It seemed like this part of my life was on its way to being mended. Having my mother on my side meant a lot.

"What are we going to do about our permits, Gram? I'm going to have to go to the stupid Sweetbriar Street Festival with him."

"I'm going with you. I don't like the way he looks at you and I never have. It's like he think he owns you and it's just a matter of time before you'll accept it. You're not dating or sleeping with that little shit to get this shop open even though he seems to think you will. We'll figure something out if it comes down to that but I'm pretty sure he knows better than to directly threaten you with the permits."

"I don't know, Gram. I think he might try."

"Play along for now unless he goes farther than you can handle. Pretend you're the pretty dumb blonde he wants you to be until we get what we need. We'll spread the word after the shop is open. No woman deserves to be intimidated by the likes of him. Does that work for you?"

I didn't want to be around him but didn't want to create another issue if I didn't have to. "Yeah, that's what I was thinking."

"Are you two talking about Jared? He would never do such a thing," Mom scoffed. "I've known him since he was a baby, for goodness's sake."

"*Ugh*. I'm so sick of you defending him and trying to get me to like him! I am not interested in dating him, mother."

Her head drew back on her neck in confusion. "It's been years since I wanted you to go out with Jared, honey. You know that."

"Um no, I do *not* know that. I know no such thing. What about Valentine's Day? I had to hide in the back room of Vi's shop for her entire party while you repeatedly texted to tell me he was there. Lily said—"

"I was texting to tell you he was there, yes. But to warn you to stay in the back. His intentions toward you have been clear since you got back to Sweetbriar. He's always had a crush on you, and I know you aren't interested in him that way."

"So, Lily misunderstood when she told me you were trying to get me to go out with him. Is that what you're saying?"

"It seems like it. I'm sorry, darling. I should have gone back there myself to warn you, but he was being so chatty I didn't want him to follow me. Don't get me wrong. Back in your high school days, Marjorie had me convinced it would be cute for the two of you to be together and for a while I agreed with her. But that's not where your interests were, and I told her so. You had an adventurous spirit and you deserved to discover it without a boyfriend holding you back. But then you got involved with that

Owen and got engaged and we all know how that turned out, the cheater. Those good looks are completely wasted on the likes of him, sad isn't it?"

"Dahlia," Gram snapped. "Leave her alone. Jared is a pest and always has been, always running after Holly at school and whenever he was over at the house with his mama. Who do you think told her to punch him in the nose when he kept tugging on her braids? Me, that's who. That whole 'boys will be boys, shoving girls around on the playground' stuff is bullshit and I let her know how to stick up for herself." Gram stood, took my hand, and lifted her chin, like *I got this*. Mom always had a blind spot when it came to Jared.

"Nonsense. He was just a shy little boy with a crush. But I hope he isn't trying to use his position to get close to you. That isn't right and we will not tolerate it if it's the case. Just please consider giving him the benefit of the doubt. Remember, he's the one who told you about Owen's cheating. He saved you from making a huge mistake. He wouldn't have done that if he was so bad, right?"

"I remember, okay? I know I owe him." I hated feeling indebted to him. It made it hard to set boundaries.

"You do not own him a thing, Holly. Dahlia, do not use the fact that he told her what anyone else in her life would have told her if they had known. Do not to try to make her like that boy," Gram insisted. "Holly, any decent person would have told you Owen was cheating on you."

"Are you two about to argue now? Isn't that ironic?" I

joked to lighten the mood. I didn't want them fighting on my behalf. Especially because I was going to do whatever the hell I wanted anyway.

"Hush," they said in unison, and I laughed.

Chapter 14
Liam

Halfway to Luke's office I realized what I'd done and turned around. I'd left Holly and Rosemary alone in that house after Owen had put his hands on her. Clouded with anger, I had stormed out to find Luke and get that asshole officially fired, possibly arrested, and out of Holly's life in every way I could think of. Never had I done something this stupid. But I also had never felt anger quite like this before and I didn't want her to see me this way. I can't believe I had left them there unprotected.

What if he came back? His behavior was like nothing I'd seen from him before.

I flipped a U-turn and headed back to make sure they were okay. I passed Jared in his Porsche when I turned onto Rosemary Street, the flashy prick. There was another asshole I had my eye on. Something about him had rubbed me the wrong way from day one.

Pulling into the driveway, I recognized Dahlia's

minivan parked at the curb, and no sign of Owen's truck. I breathed a sigh of relief. Maybe I hadn't entirely fucked up and they were okay.

"Liam, sweetheart!" Dahlia's beaming face greeted me as I walked up the path to the front porch. "We're headed to Holloway's for burgers. Join us? I'm driving."

"Burgers for breakfast?"

Holly shrugged and sent me a smile. "We had a craving," she said.

"I already ate, but thank you. Are you okay? I can't believe I left you two there like that. I am so sorry."

"We're fine, honey. I have my knitting needles." Rosemary patted her handbag. "If he came back, I'd have been ready for him."

Dahlia looked confused. "What? What are you talking about?"

Holly huffed a laugh. "I'll tell you over burgers, Mom. And it's okay, Liam. I mean, I can't believe he did what he did but I'm fine. I think he might have been drunk or on something. He was never rough with me before. Like, he turned out to be an idiot and a cheater, but he was never a violent asshole, you know?"

I nodded. "He won't bother you again. I'll make sure of it."

"Honestly, I'm not worried about him. His face after you threw his ass through the door spoke volumes. He won't be coming anywhere near me."

I grabbed her hand. "Come with me."

"Oh! All right, I'm coming." She gestured for Dahlia

and Rosemary to wait for her as I pulled her into the garage for some privacy.

"Me and you, Holly—" My voice was a desperate growl. He could have seriously hurt her and I couldn't stand that I hadn't been here. I tipped my head back in frustration, unsure of what to say now that I'd brought her in here. Her nearness made my senses spin and the fact that I could have lost her drove me crazy.

"Hey," she whispered and ran her hands up my chest to cup my cheeks in her palms. She searched my eyes. "I'm okay, shh. It's okay, he's gone. It's over now."

I shook my head. "No. It isn't. Look—this is not pretend, me and you. This isn't a game I'm playing. With the holidays and the going slow and—"

"What are you talking about? I'm not playing a game either. I wouldn't do that—"

"You're mine." I tried to keep the possessive desperation out of my voice, but if her sharp intake of breath was any indication I don't think I completely succeeded. "You've been mine this entire time and you know it. If he lays so much as a fingertip on you again, I'll kill him, and you know that too. This is not me being jealous. This is me protecting you. He's bad news, Holly—"

"Shh, I know." Her eyes blazed into mine. "He scared me, I admit it. And you're a protective type of man. You found me in the woods and took care of me—I haven't forgotten about that. You wish you were here today to step in too, don't you?" I nodded briefly in answer. "I know you care about me, and I know you'll keep me safe if it came down to it. You take care of people, Liam, it's what you do, and I get that. I love that about you. And I also know you're aware I went through something before coming back to Sweetbriar and how much it scared me. But I don't want you to think that's why—" She bit her lip and looked away from me as she hesitated to complete her thought.

"What? Go on. Tell me."

Her eyes shot to mine. "That's not why I want you, okay? That's not—why I'm yours."

"Sunshine, I know that. But I really like hearing you say it."

"Well, now what are we supposed to do?"

I shrugged. "Can I kiss you, just once? Then we can go back to going slow again. Maybe I'll find a holiday we can get lost in."

She nodded, her cheeks reddening as her eyes shifted to the side. "We need the same things, Liam. Please believe that. I know what you want, and I want it too."

"Do you, sunshine? I don't think you have any idea. I want a lot when it comes to you. One kiss will never be enough. But I can wait. I'll wait forever if that's what it takes to have you."

Slipping my hand around the nape of her neck, I pulled her into me. The pulse at the base of her throat beat rapidly against my thumb as I drew her face up to mine.

"What are you waiting for?" she breathed. We were inches apart, sharing the same air. I was so close to getting what I'd asked for but couldn't seem to take it. "I'm right here, Liam. Take what you need."

I crushed my mouth to hers. The touch of her lips sent a shockwave through my entire body. It was necessary, fucking essential, to feel her like this. The cold tension that had burrowed inside of my chest dissipated as I felt her melt against me, gripping my forearms to hold herself up. I swept an arm around her waist, digging my fingertips against her hip. "I got you," I groaned against her lips.

"Yes, you do," she affirmed. "You know you do. You were right about that."

I broke the kiss. "They're waiting for you." Reluctantly, I let her go.

"Yeah, I should get back out there."

I reached behind myself and opened the door, stepping aside so she could reenter the house.

Rosemary shot us a knowing grin. "All done for now?"

"Yes, ma'am." She laughed at my response.

Dahlia checked her phone. "Holly, an officer just picked Owen up. We can talk about what to do about him over breakfast."

"I'm going to get to work then," I told them. "Enjoy your breakfast, ladies."

"I'll be back soon, Liam. Will I be in the way if I start bringing some of my supplies into the house to sort through?"

I shook my head. "Not at all. You can put it in the kitchen, and I'll transfer it to the work room when I finish in there if you like."

"That would be perfect. See you later."

I waved as they got into Dahlia's van and left. Then I headed inside to get to work finishing up the floor installation Owen had been working on.

A while later, I was on my hands and knees installing a baseboard when I heard the front door open. Footsteps sounded across the floor behind me. I knew it was Holly, but she didn't say a word. She just stopped, silently watching me as I worked.

"I can feel your eyes all over me, sunshine."

"The, uh, floor is looking good. And you installed the counter too? You're amazing. Oh hell, you look hot bent over like that. You can really work a baseboard, Liam. Is there a make out day, or a no pants day, or a get into bed with your crush day coming up that we could exploit now that we're back to going slow?"

I stood, took the few steps that separated us and swung her into the circle of my arms. "Actually, No Pants Day *is* coming up, so is Lover's Day, and I Don't Want to Wait Day. Zipper Day is pretty soon, too. We could unzip and celebrate early?"

"I like I Don't Want to Wait Day, it feels right for us."

"I think so too. But first, I have to say this again with a clear head. I'm sorry about losing my temper and storming out of here. And if I was a little too demanding earlier, I'm sorry for that as well. I worked most of my anger out hammering in the baseboards while you were gone, and I feel like shit about how I handled things."

She placed a finger to my lips to hush me. "Don't be sorry, Liam. No man has ever stood up for me like that. To be honest, I loved everything about it." Her eyes dropped to my chest and she sounded a little sheepish when she said, "I don't know what this says about me, but it turned me on when you threw him out the door. Does that make me a bad person?"

I would have laughed at her response but I was distracted by the creamy expanse of her neck where a pink flush was slowly rising. "No, he deserved it."

"'Kay . . ." She squirmed in my arms to get closer. "I still haven't run to the store for condoms. We'll have to tone down the I Don't Want to Wait Day celebration unless you bought some. Did you?"

"I have not, and it is utterly stupid of me. So No Pants and Zipper Days are also off the table. But that's okay because we're taking this slow like we need to do. Plus I still have to open a few doors, hold your hand, and take you to dinner, remember?"

That blush rose to color her cheeks and I smiled as her eyes shifted up to gaze into mine. "Oh, yeah. We wouldn't want your grandma to have to haunt you, right?"

"That's right, baby." Damn, she was pretty. Her dark lashes fluttered down as she inhaled a soft breath. Every time I got close to her like this, I noticed something new. The light dusting of freckles across the bridge of her nose, or the dimple on her left cheek, or the irresistible way her lips had just parted as she waited for me to kiss her.

"Liam . . ." Her breath feathered across my lips. "Please . . ."

"I'm taking you out Friday, sunshine."

"God, yes. But kiss me again today?"

My heart hammered in my chest as I pressed my mouth to hers. What I wanted, needed, and would die to have was wrapped up in this stunning woman standing in my arms. Overwhelmed by her nearness, everything faded into the background as I slid my tongue against hers and pulled her tighter.

She'd been running through my mind on a perpetual loop since I'd met her. The further we went, the deeper I fell. Those gorgeous lips, then the way she kissed me. Those pretty eyes, then the way she looked at me. The more I tried to keep her out of my mind, the more I fucking *had* to think about her. And I knew once I got inside of her, I'd never want to leave.

Her arms draped over my shoulders as her fingers threaded into my hair, holding on, tugging me close while she peppered soft little kisses to my jaw then down my throat, ending at the exposed skin above my collar. "I love how you kiss me. Like you can't get enough," she whispered as she unbuttoned my shirt and spread it apart to kiss her way across my chest.

"Because your mouth tastes like heaven." I let my fingers slide into her soft blonde hair to pull her face up to mine. "Do you have any idea how much I want you? What you do to me?" I didn't wait for an answer; I held her chin steady in the palms of my hands and slammed my mouth back to hers with a groan.

I wanted to worship her entire body with my mouth, but I knew we wouldn't get that far, not today. So I settled for letting my hands roam. Down the back of her neck, along the graceful arch of her spine and lower to grip her gorgeous ass in my palms. It fit perfectly into my hands as if she were made exactly for me. I lifted and she gave a little hop, wrapping her legs around my waist as I walked us to the rear of the space to set her on the edge of the shop's new counter.

"Yes . . ." She wrapped me tight and scooted forward, pressing our hips together with a little grind as she darted her tongue out and flicked it against the base of my throat.

"You're so fucking sexy, Holly. I can't wait to get inside you." I banded an arm around her hips to yank her closer and took her mouth again.

"I don't know if I want you to keep talking or shut up and kiss me some more," she mumbled against my lips.

I nudged her backward and kissed a path down her neck, grinning when she reached between us to unzip her hoodie and there was nothing underneath.

I groaned. "So pretty . . ." With a surge forward, I sucked one perfect pink nipple into my mouth, teasing the hardening tip with my tongue.

Her head fell between her shoulder blades as her back arched. Her hair spread like sunbeams over the counter, and I buried a hand in that soft mass of waves to wind it around and around my fist as I held her tight and moved to her other breast to give it the same attention.

Enveloping her body with mine, I buried my face in her neck and inhaled her sweet scent. She smelled like citrus and jasmine. Like amber, musk, and something that was inherently Holly. She was sunshine. She was light, and love, and I wanted to devour her. I had never wanted a woman in my life like I wanted this one. I needed her. I couldn't imagine my life without her in it, and maybe that was the difference.

"Liam, I need more." Her breathy little moan shot straight to my cock, so I pressed it hard between her legs, letting her feel what she did to me, groaning against her lips as she pulled me tighter with her feet on my ass and writhed against me.

Taking my hand from her hair, I grabbed her by the hips and jammed my knee against the side of the counter as I slid her down to straddle my thigh. "Use me." My voice was an unrecognizable, guttural growl. "Get yourself off on me. I've imagined this since we woke up together with all that soft wet heat pressed against my leg. I have to see it. I need it, Holly."

Hot eyes met mine, flashing blue fire as she tilted her hips back and widened her stance. Her perfect tits flattened against my upper abs as she gripped the sides of my open shirt. I held her hips, fingertips digging into her round ass to keep her steady as she rode my thigh, grinding herself against me, sliding up and down, and pressing hard as she worked herself to release with her eyes never once leaving mine. "Is this what you wanted to see?" She asked before she bit her lip and threw back her head.

"Yes. Don't stop. You are so fucking gorgeous right now. I want to watch you come apart on me."

She quickened her pace and arched her back. "Touch me."

"Touch you? Tell me where, tell me what you want,

and I'll do it. I'd die for the pleasure of having my hands on your body. Do you know that? Not being inside of you right now is torture, Holly. Beautiful fucking torture, but we're not stopping until you make yourself come. Do you understand?"

Her lips parted on a moan as she nodded, eyes closed, hair flowing behind her in a shimmering blonde river as her body tensed, ready to fall apart.

I brushed a thumb over a dusky pink nipple, then pinched it gently, laughing darkly as she moaned. "Is that what you needed, sunshine?" I'd lost my mind over her. I was nothing but desperate burning need, more turned on than I've ever been in my life despite knowing I wasn't going to get inside her today. That's what Holly Barrett did to me.

"Yes . . ." Her face flushed a deep rose red, and her breath came in a long surrendering moan as she bowed forward to press her open mouth to my chest before she let go, coming in shuddering waves with her thighs clamped on mine.

"My legs are shaking." Her breathy laugh tickled my chest as she wrapped her arms around my waist and held on. "Oh my god," she whispered against my bare skin.

I kissed the top of her head and gathered her close. "I got you."

"I know you do. I've never come that hard in my life. What even was that?"

"It was fucking beautiful is what it was."

"It was all you. You do things to me, Liam."

I stroked her back as she came down, trembling and clutching at my shirt. "It was my pleasure."

"Not yet it wasn't." She reached for the button of my jeans.

"We can't—"

"Move that leg so I can get on my knees, Liam. There's still plenty we can do together until our Friday."

I couldn't refuse. After making sure she was steady, I stepped back, and she stood up. I wanted her naked almost as much as I didn't. The way her nipples peeked out of that open hoodie as she moved was sexy as hell.

She was down on her knees with her hands on my zipper when the doorbell rang.

"Are you kidding me?" she hissed.

I helped her up and hastily buttoned my fly, then my shirt as she zipped up her hoodie with a scowl.

"Holly, it's Jared." The door was steel, but his pounding echoed throughout the ground floor. "Come to the door," he shouted. "I have something for you."

"Fricking damn it," she grumbled and ran a hand through her hair as she stomped to the door and threw it open. "What?" she demanded to a shocked looking Jared.

Chapter 15
Holly

I was finally about to get a taste of Liam and this jackass had to knock on my door. My temper boiled over as I glared at Jared, standing there holding a huge bouquet of roses, a manila envelope, and what remained of his smile.

"I'm sorry." Smoothing my expression into something resembling friendly, I gestured for him to step into the foyer.

Liam was here so I wasn't worried about things getting awkward with Jared. Well, at least for me. He could feel as awkward as he wanted but as long as he wasn't hitting on me, what did I care?

"Did I catch you at a bad time?" His eyes darted past me to scan the open space of the ground floor. Probably trying to see if I was alone.

"No. Liam was just showing me the progress he made while I was gone. It's fine. What can I do for you?"

"I brought you these. The first of your permits have

been approved. You can now sell tea and other non-alco-holic beverages, along with prepared food."

Liam crossed to the foyer to join us, snatching the envelope from Jared's hand. "This should be delivered to the McCabe Construction office. Not to Holly and not here. Luke is handling all the preliminary approvals for her and Rosemary through his company. But you already knew that, didn't you?"

"Sure, I realize that. But I thought I'd stop by and offer my congratulations in person." He passed the roses to me. "We go back years, don't we, Holly?" He shot a glare to Liam. "There's no need for formality between friends, is there?"

"I mean, I don't know anything about permits and stuff. Luke takes care of that so . . ." I gestured to the envelope, hesitant to be harsh with him when apparently there were more permits waiting for approval. "Luke should probably have this. But yeah, we've known each other since kindergarten so I guess it's okay this time." I set the roses on the built in shelf adjacent to the front door. "These are pretty. Thank you."

"Of course." He cleared his throat. I knew he wanted to say more but I didn't want to hear it. He probably wanted to talk about the Street Festival, but yeah, no thank you. I tried to keep my face neutral, but I must have failed because he flinched and took a step back. "I guess I'll get going. Uh, see you soon, Holly."

"Bye." I slammed the door behind him. "Unfreaking-believable."

A low laugh rumbled from Liam's chest. "I didn't like

him before and I sure as hell can't stand him now," he announced.

"Yeah, and I'm sorry, but I'm not in the mood anymore," I declared. "He wrecked it and I'm pissed."

"It's probably for the best." He dragged a hand over his beard. "I was already having a hard time coming to terms with not being able to, uh . . ."

A sideways grin quirked up my lips. "Cross the finish line and fuck us both stupid?"

"Yup, that," he chuckled.

I took a deep breath. "Okay, I have a new plan. You do what you gotta do here. I'm going to the Quickbriar Stop and Go to pick up the essentials, okay?"

"Yes, ma'am."

I gave him a saucy smile and sauntered toward him. I hooked my finger through his belt loop and said, "Friday night, Liam. No more holidays and no more waiting, okay?"

"Brilliant, count me in."

"Later."

I practically ran to Lily's car, which had somehow ended up parked in my driveway. I'd ask the sibling group text who to thank for driving it over later. Right now I was on a mission.

I pulled into the lot next to a familiar looking Porsche. What is it with Porsches and all the little dick energy losers in this town? Violet's ex had one and so did fricking Jared. I bet Owen would drive one too if his stupid ass could afford it.

Yeah, I'd just gotten off spectacularly with Liam, but

it had done nothing to put me in a good mood. Especially when I knew I'd have gone off again if I could have had a go at him. His dick was huge. I'd felt it pressed against me and I couldn't wait to get my hands, mouth, and my other parts all over it.

Friday couldn't come soon enough for me.

I was frustrated in so many ways right now. I was sexually frustrated, obviously. Then there was dickhead Owen this morning and Jared and his bad timing, both of which sucked. But most of all I was frustrated with my own dumbass self for not buying condoms once I had realized that future Holly was definitely going to be getting a piece of Liam. This was not a happy combo. My mood had turned to shit.

"Holly! Babe, what a lovely surprise." Jared greeted me the second I crossed through the door while Elizabeth—my bestie, Tess's little sister—snickered behind the counter. She knew all about Jared's crush on me and how I felt about it. She and I were quite friendly too, so the vibes I was giving off were not lost on her like they were on poor oblivious, unsuspecting, pain-in-my-ass Jared.

"I'm in a bad mood right now, Jared. Headache, hangry, grumpy, I think I may even have cramps. We'll talk later." I tried to get around him, but he reached out and grabbed my arm.

I stared at his hand on my arm like it was a spider I was about to squash but he didn't let go. Instead he led me further into the store. "Let's get you taken care of then, darling girl. What do you need? My treat." He grabbed one of the small grocery carts by the door and smiled expectantly at me.

What do I need? For you to get the hell out of my face and leave me alone. Is that too much to ask?

"Oh, I don't know—" An idea struck me, and I grinned. "Are you sure?" I batted my eyelashes at him like the simpleton he seemed to think I was.

"Of course, sweetie. I only want you to be happy." He brushed his fingers through the ends of my hair again. A touch without entirely touching. Seemingly innocent but so, so, *so* fucking *not*.

We had known each other forever; we'd grown up together. Our mothers had been friends for decades. But somehow, even after all this time, he still knew nothing about me. And the kicker was I didn't think he even wanted to.

"You're too kind to me." I grabbed hold of the cart and started tossing shit into it. Lots of random shit because screw him and his persistence and his never-leaving-me-alone "nice guy" bullshit. We'd see how nice he was after buying me half this damn store. I didn't feel bad, knowing he could afford it. He drove a damn Porsche for eff's sake. Maybe I could drive him away by being a pain in the ass.

"Retail therapy. I love it." He chuckled. "Get what you need. I enjoy taking care of the women in my life." He winked and brushed my hand on the cart with his pinkie. "I'm a generous boyfriend. All the ladies I've dated have said I'm a catch. Have you ever been in a Porsche, sweetie? I'd love to take you for a ride and catch up with you, show you what I have to offer. I'm a high value man now, Holly. Not the shy, quiet boy you knew back in school."

Elizabeth was making gagging noises behind the counter, but Jared was too busy fawning over himself to notice. I met her rolling eyes in the security mirror but had to look away before I started laughing.

Well, shit.

Whatever.

Once my shop was open, I was done with putting up with him.

Maybe honesty would work. It was worth a shot. "Thank you, but I can't. I'm not dating right now. Not you or anyone, okay? I've been through a lot lately. I had an incident before I got back to Sweetbriar. It was serious and I'm still trying to work my way through it. I'm not ready for—"

"Holly, that's silly and you know it. There's nothing like getting back on the horse, right? Whatever that little incident was, it's over now, isn't it? You're here, and you're more beautiful than ever. You look just fine to me. Let it go, babe. It's time to move on—that's the best thing you can do. My Porsche is right outside. I'll take you to lunch at the Riverview, you can order whatever your heart desires, and we'll get your mind off all your troubles together. Okay, babe?"

"Ummm . . ." *Wow.*

I was right. He didn't care about me one bit. Everyone in my family was practically begging me to talk to them about what happened, and meanwhile, this asshole who claimed he was my friend, kept asking to date me, and swore he wanted to get to know me better, couldn't be bothered to hear a word of it.

Elizabeth fake coughed out a, "Dick," and then cleared her throat. "Hey there, Jared," she shouted. "I see you're back to harass my customers. Misogyny is the powerhouse of the incel, am I right, Holls?"

Before I could fully process her words, I barked a laugh, then covered my mouth with a hand.

"If you weren't the only decent place in town to get gas, I would quit coming in here. You have quite the disrespectful mouth on you, Elizabeth. I do just fine with the ladies, thank you very much. You should spend more time worrying about yourself and your poor prospects rather than poking fun at good men, don't you think?"

"Whatever you say, bro." She snorted and went back to texting on her cell.

"She is unbelievable." He shook his head. "You're not still friends with her crazy sister, are you?"

"Uh, yes I am. Tess will always be my best friend."

"You should probably rethink that. But we have time to get into your friends, your choices in attire . . ." I stood there gobsmacked as his eyes ran over my hoodie and jean shorts clad body before landing back on mine. "All I'm saying is you're a true beauty. You should dress like it. And Tess, with all those kids . . ." He shook his head. "You could do better in the friend department."

I scoffed. "Um . . ."

Do not punch him in the face. Do not. Punch him. In the fricking face.

Elizabeth and I met eyes in the mirror again. "Holly," she called out. "Tess just texted me. Can you grab a pack of Pampers and bring them to her? She's out. Aunt Jen called in sick or I'd do it myself."

"Of course!" I tossed a pack in the cart and hauled my booty to the front counter. I'd hold off on picking up the condoms today. I absolutely did not want to give Jared any hope that I intended to use them with him.

"I've got this, Jared. Tess needs me. I can't go to lunch with you today."

"Raincheck?"

"We can talk about it later."

"Oh, well, I'll say my goodbyes then." He kissed my cheek and sauntered to the door.

"You don't really need all that shit, do you?" Elizabeth gestured to the cart once he'd gone through the door.

"Uh, no. Well, some of it." I grabbed the Doritos and a Diet Coke and placed them on the counter. I hesitated before adding a Hershey bar and pack of hair ties. "Be right back." I ran to the aisle where they kept the condoms and grabbed a few boxes. Variety was good, right? I pictured Liam naked with a florescent green dick then put back the colored ones; I'd rather save that image for my monster books and alone time. I dashed back to the counter to add my prophylactic assortment to my pile of goodies. "That's it. I'll put the rest of this stuff back."

"Don't worry. I'll take care of it." She shrugged and rang me up. "You provided my entertainment for the hour, you're good."

"Happy to be of service." I huffed a laugh.

"How did you manage not to slap that smug smile off his face? Please tell me. I feel like I could learn more from you than my anger management support group."

"Uh, well, I need him to approve all the permits for my shop. And our moms are friends, but you already knew that part."

She nodded sagely. "Ahh, so it's just a matter of time. I totally get that. Watch out for him though. He's a wannabe heartbreaker. He's basically a giant douche bag with some bizarro agenda to find the perfect trophy wife. You should hear the shit he says when he thinks people aren't listening." She glanced at me pointedly.

The Stop and Go and Violet's shop were the two main gossip hubs in town. Every piece of Sweetbriar news filtered through both places at some point.

My blood ran cold as I contemplated her words. "What do you mean?"

"The things that go around town about you don't come from where you think they do anymore. Basically, Ava and Maren are busy living their own sad little lives now, is what I'm saying. Now, Jared on the other hand, is used to getting what he wants in this town but there is one thing he hasn't had yet, right? And that's *you.*"

"Are you saying Jared says shit about me? Why would he do that if he wants to date me?"

"I can't confirm anything yet," she answered. "But I'm pretty sure that a lot of it comes from him and it started before you left town. No one wants to date the 'Sweetbriar slut,' right? He's trying to eliminate the competition."

"Ohhhhhh, that makes so much sense, that rotten little shit. Don't say a word about this to anyone. I need him for now. But when I don't—"

She snickered at my tone. "Lord help that motherfucker when you don't need him. Am I right?"

"Damn straight. *Ugh!*"

Thankfully, I made it home without rage-speeding or finding Jared to run him over. Liam's truck was gone when I got here. After pulling into the garage, my phone pinged with a text.

> LIAM: A pipe burst on one of Luke's projects. I'll be working with him today. When you get home, lock up, set the alarm, and don't let anyone but family in. Okay?

Protective or bossy?

I decided he was protective and let the warm tingles flow through me along with a *squee* of satisfaction that I had a man in my life who actually cared about me. Unlike Jared, the piece of crap dumbass who thought I was stupid enough to fall for his shit.

> ME: Yes, sir. LOL

> LIAM: Good girl. If I don't see you
> tonight, know that I'm knee deep in a
> flooded warehouse with Luke.

Good girl?

Why was that so hot?

And why was I contemplating ways to get him to say that phrase out loud? A shiver ran through me as I unlocked the interior door and headed into the kitchen.

I spent the rest of the day going through my boxes of supplies for the shop. Oils, herbs I'd ordered to use until I had enough of what I had grown in the garden, along with all the things I would need to package them up covered the counter as I sorted through my purchases. Then I gathered my laptop and a notebook to make lists and plans for a menu. I wanted my shop to be more than somewhere to just buy stuff; I wanted it to be a gathering place as well. Rosemary's Apothecary was shaping up to be just the thing I needed.

Time flew as I worked. Next thing I knew, it was nighttime and I was starving. The sheer curtains in the kitchen did nothing to hide the dark outside and I shivered as I imagined what could be lurking outside the house while I was in here all alone like a sitting duck.

Or a hiker by herself in a flimsy tent.
Alone.
Dark.

I couldn't decide if I should run upstairs and hide, get

in my car and leave, or call someone to come here and be with me. None of it sounded good. So I sat at the table keeping vigil at the window, staring into the dark and waiting for something to happen as my panicked imagination ran wild.

Suddenly my cell rang, breaking me out of whatever freaked-out trance I'd fallen into. I fumbled for it, cursing as it skidded across the table.

It was Asher, the oldest of my siblings. I checked the time. It was exactly nine PM. He called to check on me and tell me goodnight every night because he knew I needed it.

"Hello. Ash?" I burst into tears, unable to cope with the intrusive thoughts that had taken over my mind. "Can you come get me?"

Chapter 16
Holly

Okay, so technically last Sunday was my first and *only* night at the house. And I didn't even sleep until it was daylight, after Liam had tucked me in.

I'd been crashing at Asher's place for the last couple days. It was embarrassing and I didn't want anyone to know.

I was scared of the dark, afraid to be alone, and drowning in the humiliation of it all. I was hoping I could spend a few nights here with Ash and get my head together before anyone had to find out what a chickenshit I had become.

Asher was the one sibling I had who would never say a word about anything to anyone, ever. Sometimes I wondered how many of our secrets he knew, but it would be pointless to ask because he'd never tell. He was divorced, so there was no wifey around to spill my beans to and Mark and Mara were with his ex for the week, so I didn't have to worry about them blabbing my scaredy-cat secret either.

I had it all covered. I got up extra early to head to the house so I could have coffee and kisses with Liam before he got to work building stuff and fixing things, and whatever else he did all day. After, I'd head over to Violet's to help her with the morning rush at the shop then go back to the house to work on my garden. Once Liam finished my work room, I'd start creating inventory.

But for now, it was dinnertime on day two of Holly's Humiliating Hideout at Asher's House Adventure and I wasn't ready to go home yet.

He and I were at his kitchen table playing poker while the food cooked. He had taught me how to make Mom's meatloaf. It wasn't as hard as I thought, but it was gross having my hands in all that ground beef. And I was correct the other day with Jude and Levi; mashed potatoes were indeed, easy.

"How long are you planning to keep this secret up?" he asked. "Not that I mind you staying here, but Mark and Mara will be back next week." Ash was as tall as Liam, but slimmer with bright red hair like Lily and Rose. He was sweet, protective, and most importantly, had an empty guest room and the ability to keep his mouth shut.

"I don't know, I'll guess I'll go home when Mark and Mara come back. They can't keep a secret worth a damn."

"You got that right. You doing okay?"

"Yeah, I'm totally fine."

His tone softened as he said, "Well, I know you're not since you're here, don't I?"

I hid my face in my hands. "I'm sorry you guys spent all that money fixing my place up—"

"You know that's not what this is about."

I jumped as someone knocked on the door. "Yo, Ash. Open up. I see your lights on."

"Crap, it's Cade!" I squealed. "I have to hide."

"Holly, open up, honey."

I cringed. "Dang it, it's dad too."

"Do you honestly believe I don't know you're in there, Holly?" Cade shouted through Ash's kitchen door.

"What the hell, Ash?" I accused. "You ratted me out?"

He put his hands up at his sides and laughed. "I didn't say anything. You're shit at being sneaky and they're both cops."

"Whatever."

I unlocked the door, and they came striding inside.

"Why are you here? Is everything okay? How are things with Liam going?" Cade peppered me with questions.

"Go easy on each other, you hear?" my dad warned us. Cade and I were known to butt heads from time to time.

I sank back into my chair and picked up my cards without answering. Ash and I were playing for M&M's, and I was winning.

"Well?" he prodded.

I glared up at him. "Oh, I don't know, things with

Liam are probably going about the same way things are going for you and your ex-wife." I offered him a saccharine-sweet smile. "How is Charlotte, by the way? And don't pretend you don't know how she is, because I have already heard otherwise from multiple sources."

He rolled his eyes and pulled out a chair. "Fine. Deal me in. Let's discuss other things—like your asshole ex, Owen. Luke fired him. Matt arrested him, but Ava has already bailed him out. I heard Liam is trying to find him to do lord knows what to him. You're pressing charges, right? Gram said he shoved you."

"Well, yeah, he did. But that was after I slugged him in the stomach and probably broke his toe. I mean, he did sneak up on me and grab my ass so technically he started it. You know how my temper is."

He laughed. "I know. You're still in therapy, right?"

"No, I quit that. I'm okay now."

Dad's eyes were gentle and contemplative. "Holly, you're sleeping at Ash's place because you can't be alone in the dark. Think about staying with your mom and me again, okay, honey?"

I wrinkled my nose. "It sounds so much worse when you put it like that," I muttered. "I'll think about it."

"Being able to slide into denial and pretend you're okay is not the same as healing," Cade added.

I snorted. "Whatever you say, Dr. Phil."

"She's deflecting." He addressed Ash and not me. "What smells so good?"

"Meatloaf."

"Awesome." Cade crossed his feet at the ankles as

Ash dealt him a hand and Dad headed into the living room to turn on the TV.

Apparently, they were staying for dinner. When Ash passed him a beer I knew for sure they were here for the evening.

Great.

Cade was the sibling who approached problems head on, and my dad would be sweet and sympathetic until I broke down and spilled my guts everywhere. I should have gone back to Levi and Jude's. There I'd be three beers deep and stuffing my face with pizza right about now instead of about to be shoved headfirst into an emotional breakthrough.

"I'm not in denial," I halfheartedly protested.

Cade leaned back in his chair. "Okay, then let's talk about what happened that night in your tent."

"Sure, Mr. Tough Love. I'll just unload everything right now."

"Defensive," he remarked to Ash, with a look of concern on his face. I knew he loved me. I also realized he was trying to help but I wasn't in the right frame of mind to accept any help. Not from him, or Dad, or anyone. I had tried therapy but saying what had happened to me out loud had only made me feel worse. Maybe I needed to talk to someone different or just suck it up and make another appointment to try again.

"Lay off her, Cade," Dad shouted from Ash's couch. "Not everyone deals with things the same way and that's okay. Sometimes peace, quiet and a little bit of time are all that's needed. But not too much time, Holly. You can't go on like this forever, honey."

Cade took a deep breath. "Okay, Dad is right, I just hate seeing you in pain, Holls. I wanted to help you. I'm sorry. And I'll admit that Charlotte has me wound up tight. I came on too strong with you. I'm really sorry if I was too harsh."

I shrugged a shoulder up. "I know you're trying to be helpful, but I can't deal with it now. Maybe it's dumb but thinking about it puts me back inside that tent in the dark and I'm just not ready to go there again."

"I'll say one more thing and then I swear I'll stop, okay?"

I put my cards down and nodded for him to continue.

"When someone wants to do you harm, you have to do whatever it takes to save your own life. I know it's hard to come to terms with, but what else could you have done? Let him hurt you?"

My eyes drifted to the table as I forced myself to keep listening.

"You did the right thing. If you take only one thing from what I said tonight, please let it be that. You did what you had to do and I'm so damn happy you're still around."

I nodded "Okay. I heard you. I promise."

"Good," he chuckled. "Because I wasn't finished yet. You've always been independent and pretty fucking fearless too. You traveled all over the world alone. That night shook you. It reframed how you see yourself." I opened my mouth to respond but he held up a hand. "Don't answer. Just listen. I know you're struggling because I've been there. I know how it feels to have to fight for your life and what you have to do to win. We can talk about it whenever you want. The memories are going to keep haunting you, Holly. They won't stop until you're ready to face them."

Maybe his words held more weight because he was a cop. Or maybe because he was my big brother. Or just maybe, as each day passed, I was more ready to hear the encouragement everyone in my life was trying to give me because what he'd said penetrated the shield I'd built up over the last few months. But I still didn't want to talk about it.

"I want to talk about it—someday. I just can't right now. Okay?"

Cade offered me a sympathetic smile. "I get that. Believe me, I do. I love you, Holly and I'm here to help. You can come to me any time and I promise I'll try to stop being so pushy."

I had to lighten the mood, so I did what I always do and made a joke. "I love you too but we both know you can't stop being pushy. It's in your nature, never gonna happen."

He lifted his shoulders in a sheepish shrug. "That's fair."

I also doubled down and pushed back because I knew he was having a hard time too. "You know I'm here for you to talk to as well."

He nodded with a suspicious grin etched across his features.

"So, Charlotte's back in town, huh? Let's get back to that. How are you?" Cade's ex-wife was the very definition of the one who got away and since I was the definition of someone who needed to change the subject, I decided to turn the tables on his pushy butt.

A warning cloud spread across his features. "How about we talk about her right after we talk about you and why you're crashing here instead of your new place. Or maybe you and Liam? Take your pick."

I laughed because Cade and I would never stop pushing each other's buttons; it was our favorite thing to do. This fact had been made abundantly clear over the years. Everyone in our family would swear we didn't get along, but we did. "Whatever, maybe we should talk about Ash instead. Why are you still single, Asher?" We could also turn on a dime and tag-team our siblings. We were two sides of the same coin, which was probably why we butted heads sometimes.

Ash peered at me over his cards and shook his head like he couldn't believe my traitorous ways.

"Yeah, man," Cade piped in. "Why *are* you still single? You've been divorced longer than you were married. It's time to get back out there."

"Kids!" Dad's warning shout traveled into the kitchen over the din of the game he was watching on TV. But like usual, we ignored him.

"Ooh, Cade! Maybe he should hire a nanny. I just finished reading this book about a single dad and a nanny that was pretty hot. I mean, you're not a billionaire or a rancher, Ash, but you could still meet a nice lady that way. And bonus! She'll get along with the kids."

Ash shook his head, aiming a scowl across the table at me and Cade. "I—no. I'm not talking about this. I'd rather play in awkward silence while we wait for the meatloaf to cook."

"Okie dokie." I exchanged a sideways glance with Cade, who let out a snicker.

Ash laid down his cards, in reality and metaphorically. He was done with this conversation and about to end it. "I don't want to try again yet and there's nothing wrong with that. My focus is on Mark and Mara and being a good dad, as it should be. I swear, you two are the hot messes right now and yet somehow, I'm the butt of the joke. How is that?"

"You're the oldest. Maybe that's why." I shrugged.

"Yep," Cade agreed. "That's it. You can take it."

Ash snorted then stood up to check the meatloaf. He called out, "Food is done," just as my phone pinged with a text.

"You know what? This is my last night here. I'm going home in the morning," I declared, feeling a sudden surge of bravery. I was an adult, I had been taking care of myself for years, and I could do hard things, damn it.

"I wasn't trying to chase you out, Holly. The kids won't be back until the beginning of next week. You have time," Ash said gently.

"Oh, I know that," I reassured him. I want to do this, I have to. Plus, Liam just texted. He's done for the day. He finished my work room and I want to unpack all the supplies that came in yesterday and get to work. I can do this."

"Hell yes you can," Cade agreed. "And all of us are just a phone call away."

We talked through dinner. It didn't escape my notice that they were building me up and encouraging me the entire time we spoke. By the time I got into bed, I was pumped up and ready for morning.

After waking up, I said bye to Ash, got into Lily's car and left. I hadn't even bothered to change clothes; I was still in my sleep shorts and tank from the night before. I'd shower, make coffee, do adulty things, then get busy unpacking my work room while I waited for Liam to show up for the day.

I pulled into my garage and entered from the internal door that led into the kitchen. Liam was sitting at the table. His face fell when he noticed what I was wearing. "I was here late. I came back after I loaded up the boxes of your supplies, they're in the work room ready to go. I waited for you. I probably shouldn't have stayed, but I couldn't make myself leave. I guess I had to know the truth."

"Thank you, um for doing that . . ." I breathed. The expression on his face tore at my heart.

What had he been thinking all night?

"I probably don't have the right to be hurt that you didn't come home. It's not like we were actually dating each other yet, right?"

"I, uh, Liam, this is not what you think it is."

"But I really don't have the right to *think* anything, do

I? We're not even in a real relationship. I don't have any type of claim on you, or your time, or where you spend the night. I have no right to even ask you where you were all night, do I?"

"You have every right to think about me, and ask me questions, Liam."

"We even talked about this. Holiday hall passes aren't real. I just thought—"

"Stop." Desperately clinging to the small shred of hope he wasn't assuming the worst of me, I cut him off before he could finish. But I had to know the truth, didn't I? "What did you think? Tell me," I demanded.

"I think I should have known better than to wait around for you all night. Trust doesn't come easy for me anymore. And you—"

"No. You know what? I changed my mind. I don't want to hear any more." I held up a hand. "Maybe *I* should have known better. Maybe I shouldn't have come back to Sweetbriar. So much for Friday night, right? Why even bother now." My slutty, heartbreaker Holly reputation had come back to slap me in the face again, and it killed me that he was the one to hit me with it. "Nothing ever seems to work out the way I want it to here. I don't know what I was thinking."

"You're right, you deserve better." He stood up. "I should just go."

"Wait a minute. Stop. What do you mean *I* deserve better? Explain to me why you're upset."

Was this even about me at all?

I had a sudden, nagging feeling that it wasn't, and I refused to lose him over a misunderstanding.

His eyes met mine, stricken and sad. "For a second, when you first walked in, I did think you'd been with someone else, but it only took one more second to reject that thought. That isn't you. You aren't the type of woman who would do such a thing. You wouldn't play me."

"No, I would never do that. Thank you for realizing it," I murmured.

"I have a lot of demons in my past. I have PTSD, Holly. I almost—fuck, I tried to kill myself a few months back after my grandmother died and I don't even remember doing it. Did you know that?" His brows drew together in an agonized expression.

I nodded. I knew. My mother had brought him home out of the hospital. He had stayed at my parent's house along with Luke and Lily and the kids while he got well enough to move out again and he'd been in therapy and part of Jed's veteran support group with Luke and a few other vets in the area ever since.

This had nothing to do with my reputation. I felt terrible and selfish for thinking that it was. If nothing else, he was my friend, and I never should have jumped to conclusions about what he had been thinking. "I'm so sorry. I was at Asher's house. I was scared to be alone, and I was too embarrassed to tell anyone." My voice faded away in the hushed stillness of the kitchen.

"Not even me?" The hurt in his eyes broke my heart.

"How long have you been staying there?" He asked as if holding a raw emotion in check.

I looked away. "Since Monday after we—you know."

"I see." He let out a long, audible breath. "But you didn't come to me."

I'd hurt him by not telling him. I knew it and I wished I could go back and make a different choice. "I'm sorry I didn't tell you. I'm sorry I made you think I was here every morning when I was hiding out with Ash . . ."

"Don't be. I get it, probably better than you think I do. My whole life I've had this drive that kept me going. Always after more—do more, be more, see more. I was nonstop, you know what I mean?" His voice was emotionless, distant, and it chilled me.

A warning voice echoed in my head telling me I'd wrecked everything. "I understand. I used to be the same way."

"When I got out of the Army, I didn't have it anymore. Whatever it was that drove me was gone. Every day, I felt lost. Then I met you and finally wanted something again. I wanted you."

My heart twisted. "Liam, I want you too—"

"Yeah?" The wistful quality in his voice alarmed me. I nodded in answer, struggling with the uncertainty that had arisen between us. "Is it good that *all* I seem to want is you?"

"Oh, Liam, that simply isn't true. Look at what you've done here. This place is gorgeous because of you. You work with Luke. I mean, you two are practically brothers and Lily and the kids love you. You've built a life here in Sweetbriar. My entire family adores you."

"Maybe you're right, I don't know anymore. But what I do know is it shook me more than I felt comfortable with when you didn't come home. I'm just not ready to feel this much and I don't think I have enough left inside of me to give you. Holly, I'm not sure I can do this." He stood up to leave.

My stomach flipped. I couldn't let him leave, not like this. "Wait. Please listen."

He turned back.

"I understand how you feel, Liam. I felt it when I was hiding out at Ash's house, and honestly, I've felt it since I came back to Sweetbriar. Scared. Unworthy. Like I didn't even know myself anymore. But worst of all, I felt like I was alone in dealing with something I don't even want to think about, and I was ashamed. But none of those feelings speak the truth of who I am. That's why I came back here. And that's why I'll let you go right now."

He didn't answer.

"We're not done, Liam. I won't let you walk out of my life because of some misplaced idea that I deserve something better or because you think you're not enough for me. Not when I know we care about each other, and especially not when I know you want me exactly as much as I want you." I so desperately wanted him to understand the way I saw him, the way I felt about him. "There is *nothing* better than you, Liam. No man will ever do now that I know you exist in the world."

"Listen to you." He brushed a hand beneath his eyes. "You're too good for me."

"I am not. Hello? I just made a two-day mistake crashing with Ash, Liam, and it hurt you. I lied to you and everyone in my life about where I'd been sleeping. Nobody is perfect and being 'too good' for someone is not a real thing. Go talk to Luke or Jed, get these feelings out, and when you're ready, come back to me. I'll be here waiting for you. I promise."

"I promise I'll talk to Luke. But I can't promise I'll be back. I won't hurt you anymore than I already have."

"That's the fear talking. You'll realize it later and you'll be back. We can still have our Friday, Liam. Please," I begged.

"Goodbye, Holly." He walked away.

A cold knot formed in my stomach as I heard him engage the locks and set the alarm.

He would come back, right?

A sob shook my chest as I made my way to the work room he'd just completed for me. It was gorgeous. Brand new dark wood floors and shelves filled the room. He'd hung gauzy green curtains in the windows, while a beautiful apothecary chest sat in the corner and a battered old table sat dead center. He was talented, probably a perfectionist, and he cared enough to make this space everything I dreamed it could be. He'd listened when I described my vision and brought it to life like a dream come true.

I couldn't lose him.

But I had to give him the same grace I had just received from Asher.

And the space to figure this out on his own.

It felt like both of our traumas had come out to bash us in the face and remind us they were still around to be dealt with.

I pulled out my cell and texted my therapist for an appointment.

I texted Lily.

Then I shot a text to Cade to ask him to come over. I was finally ready for the reality check he had been offering.

Chapter 17
Liam

I drove home beating myself up inside. I knew it wasn't healthy. I knew this wasn't my fault, or even hers. It was just the place in my life I was in, and I would move past it. I hadn't lost hope. I had only lost my belief that I was any sort of ready to be in a relationship with her. When I pictured myself getting married or having a kid, actually being a husband or father, all I could see was me fucking it up with my issues.

I feared my problem had become that I didn't want to wait to be well, I only wanted to be with her. Since I met her, she was all I could think about. My goal to be healthy again was no longer for myself, it was to be with *her*. This morning had shaken me up and I didn't like the thoughts that had run through my mind when she wasn't there—the judgement, the doubt, the ugliness that had been my immediate assumption when she came home in her pajamas all mussed up from sleeping somewhere else. It wasn't fair to me or to Holly to pursue a relationship when my head still wasn't on quite straight.

I pulled around the curve to pass Luke's house and head to mine, but Lily was sitting on the swing in the outdoor sitting area off to the side of the long driveway. I had to stop, especially after she began waving at me with both hands and I could see that she was shouting. I rolled my window down to hear her calling my name.

"Oh good, you heard me." She looked relieved. "Holly texted. Park your truck and come sit with me. Jed is with Calla inside making breakfast and Luke is on his way home from dropping Dylan at school."

This family.

What could I possibly have done to deserve this?

I did what she said and joined her at the swing. "I don't know why you'd even speak to me right now after how I left her."

"Oh, shut up. You need a hug. Get over here and sit with me. I'd get up and hug you myself but . . ." She gestured to her baby bump which was almost as big around as she was tall. She was barely over five feet and carrying twin boys who were due soon.

I sat. "You couldn't reach to hug me even if you did get up," I teased." At six-six, I towered over her.

"That's fair. I'll just continue to make demands and boss you around then." I slid my arm along the back of the porch swing, and she leaned into my side.

"You're going to be okay," she whispered.

"I know." And I did know. I'd come too far to *not* be okay . . . eventually.

"Good. I know you know, but I had to make sure. I had to hear you say it out loud. And I think you needed to hear yourself say it too."

"Your faith in me helps."

"Duh, I know it does." Her eyes shone with gentle laughter in the early morning sunlight as she poked me in the side. "Admit it. I'm the big sister you always wanted."

"I'm five years older and a foot and a half taller, but okay." This was a running joke between us, and it never failed to make me smile.

"So, uh, we finally decided what to name the twins."

"Oh yeah? 'Bout time." I chuckled. "You're about to pop any day now, aren't you?"

"Yup." She rubbed her bigger-than-a-beach-ball belly bump. "It is imminent, and I can't freaking wait. You have no idea how uncomfortable this is and I'm so ready to *not* have to pee every twenty minutes. Anyway, back to the subject at hand. Baby McCabe number one will be named Easton—"

"After Luke's mom and Jed. I love that."

"And baby McCabe number two will be named Carter." I met her tear-filled gaze in surprise. "After my little brother." She nudged my arm with hers while swiping beneath her eyes with her other hand.

"Lily. I'm—" I clenched my jaw to kill the sob in my throat. "I'm honored. I don't know what to say. I—are you sure you want to do this?"

"Totally sure." Her face split into a wide grin. "This could not be more perfect. You and Luke have been brothers for years, and we have our thing, of course."

"Of course." Her teasing laughter chased my tears away and I smiled.

"And these boys will carry on all of it." She patted her belly decisively.

"I am all out of words. Or maybe there aren't any adequate enough to describe how I feel right now."

"You don't have to say anything. Just know you are part of this family forever and there is no escape for you now that names are involved. It has been made official, Liam. I have declared it so."

I felt one of the babies move against my side where she was pressed against me. "Name that one after me," I joked.

"You got it." She tried to wrap an arm around me for a sideways hug but couldn't reach across her belly. "Damn it, Liam. I owe you a big hug. Put it on my hug tab. Leaning into you just isn't good enough."

I shifted on the swing and carefully wrapped her in my arms, laughing when she still couldn't reach to hug me back and patted my sides instead. "It's on your tab," I joked.

We pulled apart then sat together watching the sunlight filter through the tall pines that both surrounded and wound their way throughout the property. "I think I messed things up with your sister today," I confessed.

"No, don't worry about that. You didn't."

"I hurt her. I know I did."

She looked at me. "You haven't. But you could if you're not careful."

"You didn't see her face when I left." I let out a sigh. "She deserves someone better than me."

"Bullshit." The word came out harsh, like the crack of a whip. It startled me into full attention and sent the argument I was mentally preparing straight out of my head. "Do you know what she said to tell you when she texted me?"

I shook my head as my heartbeat echoed in my ears and pounded hope throughout my body with every beat.

"Give yourself grace, Liam. That's what she said."

Grace.

"I don't know if I can do that when no matter what you say, I *know* I've messed things up between us—"

"But you have to. There isn't any other way to get through this life, and you know it. Are any one of us perfect? Is Holly perfect?"

I turned when I heard boots crunching through the gravel at the side of the driveway.

"She's right." Jed agreed. He had baby Calla in his arms. He took a seat in one of the Adirondack chairs across from the swing with a pointed look aimed my way. "Not a single person on this planet is perfect. We all make mistakes, get scared, run away, say things we don't mean. Shit happens, Liam."

"My dad used to say that. *Shit happens, son . . .*" I let out a sad laugh. "I joined the Army because of him. I wanted to be like him and—"

"And are you like him?" Jed asked, cutting me off.

"I don't know. I was just a kid when he died."

"I remember you talking about him at the last group meeting. He was near perfect as far as you were concerned, wasn't he?" he asked casually as he bounced a giggling baby Calla on his knee and made funny faces at her. "Pretty tough thing to live up to, if you ask me."

Lily took hold of my hand above her shoulder and gave it a squeeze.

"You're pretty sneaky, old man." Luke chuckled as he approached us from his truck. I'd been so lost in thought I hadn't heard him drive up. "Dropping truth bombs, making him connect the dots like that. You're a perfectionist, Liam. You're too hard on yourself, man, and it's time to let that shit go."

"How?"

"Grace," Lily answered, as if giving myself grace was that simple. "We love you. Let us." Her mouth curved with tenderness, and I had to look away, it was too much.

"I do—"

"You belong in this family, Liam," she insisted. "I keep saying it, but I know that inside you brush my words away. You are one of us, and that means you are allowed to make mistakes and we will forgive you. You're allowed to be afraid, to be vulnerable, to have doubts, and we will still love and accept you. I don't think you get that."

I shook my head because no, I did not. I also couldn't seem to allow myself to let what she said sink in, and I couldn't find the words to explain to her, or even myself, why that was.

"Well, quit being so stubborn and quit being so damn grateful and you will. You have no need for gratitude,

Liam. We love you. Yes, I'm *grateful* I have a big, loving family, but I belong to them, and they belong to me, and we don't owe each other anything except love. Like, I'm grateful to God or the universe or whatever it was that put them into my life. But I'm not grateful to *them* because they're just as lucky to have me. Don't you see? *We* are lucky to have *you*. Promise me you'll think about what I said. Please."

"I promise." My voice sounded like it had come from somewhere outside of my body as my stomach clenched tight with an intense mixture of hope and fear.

"He promised," Luke said with a grin as he smacked a hand on my upper back. "That means it's as good as done. The perfectionist in him won't allow him to drop this until he knows exactly what he means to all of us. Right, Liam?"

I huffed a laugh, thankful to him for breaking the mood and pulling me out of the spiral of emotions I was about to drown in. "You're a smartass."

"Well, I'm emotional," Lily announced as she fanned a hand in front of her face. "And I'm starving and pregnant and I'm gonna burst if I don't get to the bathroom real fast. I need food and Kleenex and I should probably carry a Port-a-Potty around with me. *Gah!* Someone help me off this dang swing and let's go eat."

"On it." Luke gently swept her into his arms.

"That's why I came out here," Jed told her. "Breakfast is done, honey. I made everything you wanted, too."

"Biscuits and gravy?" she shouted over Luke's shoulder.

"Yup."

"Grits with grape jelly and bacon? And don't you dare laugh at me Lucas McCabe, I know it's weird."

I heard him tell her softly, "I would never laugh at you, baby."

"You're carrying my great-grandbabies, darlin'," Jed shouted. "That means you get anything you want and it's all at the table waiting on you."

"I love you, Jed!"

"You too, sweetheart." He turned to me, studying my face with his sharp-eyed gaze. "It's starting to sink in now, isn't it? You belong here, Liam. You're one of us."

"Maybe a little bit," I admitted.

"Well, let it in all the way, son. She's not gonna stop getting after you until you accept it. You know that, right?"

"I know it."

He nodded. "Then let's go eat. There's a whole lotta food that doesn't go together in there waiting for us."

"Unka Leem," Calla reached for me when Jed stood.

"See?" He passed her into my arms with a grin. "Everyone knows you belong here, even the babies. Everyone but you. You're part of this family." He patted my shoulder. "You'll get there."

I followed him inside for breakfast. As we ate, I reflected on what Lily had said, letting the words touch my heart instead of sweeping them away like she'd accurately accused me of.

I spent the rest of the day fishing with Luke in the part of the Sweetbriar River running through the rear of his property, out past my place. We didn't talk much, and I was grateful for the quiet quality time. It gave me the space to think.

And I had to get my head clear before I spoke to Holly again.

Chapter 18
Holly

I had done all the things I was supposed to do. I had an appointment with my therapist next week, damn it. I had spent time talking to Cade about everything. He'd just left for the night because I was feeling hopeful and thought I'd be okay.

But I wasn't okay.

It was dark.

The blackness outside my window had closed in on me again and I was a wreck.

Deep breaths were overrated when one is in the midst of an anxiety attack, I spitefully decided. Stupid air, refusing to get into my lungs.

I panted. Shallow breaths were amazing.

My living room swirled around me as voices filled my head like the monotonous mumblings in a Charlie Brown cartoon.

"Holly, are you okay?"

Obviously not. I shook my head and tried to take another stupid breath, coughing when I choked on air.

Well, maybe I was okay, just a little bit. As far as anxiety attacks went, this one was about a three on the Holly Barrett scale of panic-induced self-treachery. This was the first one I'd had in months, and it was already almost over.

"Anxiety is a liar. Anxiety is a liar." I repeated in my brain as I tried to get a grip on the out-of-control thoughts telling me that the fetal position on the floor in front of the sofa was the greatest place to be ever.

"She's having an anxiety attack." Luke's oh-so-helpful voice echoed in my ears.

No shit.

I'd had a couple a year since I was a kid and for no good reason either. At least nothing that had ever made sense, anyway. Okay, that wasn't true; they always made sense. I didn't like to face things. Dealing with my problems was my least favorite thing to do, especially when digging a brain hole and burying them deep worked eighty percent of the time. It was that other twenty percent I had to watch out for. That was the stuff that kept me up at night and stared at me through dark windows.

Apparently, all the changes I'd been through lately and their accompanying intrusive thoughts had combined their efforts to come at me and say hello tonight.

Not to mention the noises I'd heard and the shadows under the backyard lights. I had simply freaked myself out and was now paying the consequences. *Ugh.*

Luke's dog, Rocky, wagged his tail on the floor in front of me, occasionally barking to let everyone know how messed up I was.

And of course, Liam was here. *Of course.*

The anxious look on his face told me he knew. He knew what I was going through right now, and it was killing him as much as it was killing me that I was the one in the middle of it. I mean, when you locked eyes with your nightmares, it was a profound experience.

"Let's give her some room," Luke suggested. "It looks like she's coming out of it." Ever since we were kids, he'd been good at helping me calm down, just like my brothers and sisters.

Rocky stretched out along my side and nuzzled my cheek as they sat on the couch to give me space. Then he nudged my ear then licked my mouth. *God, I wish it were Liam lying at my side, nudging my ear and licking my mouth.* And on that weird thought, I came out of it.

"Good boy," I rasped, wrapping my arms around him and snuggling into his soft fur. "I'm okay now." Maybe I should get a dog from Jed. Or a cat. Clearly, I was feeling better if I was thinking in coherent sentences and contemplating pet ownership. "Thanks, Luke."

"Yeah, of course." He held out a hand and helped me up to sit on the couch. "How long has this been going on?"

"Um, I had one when I first got back home. And now this one. I hate this." I couldn't seem to raise my voice above a whisper, but they heard me.

"I hate them too," he confessed.

"Yup." Liam added and his deep timbered voice sent a thrill up my spine despite my screwed-up situation.

"Ugh, you too?"

Was he back in my life?

Or was he just here because Luke was? And why were they here anyway?

His gaze was steady and kind as he studied my face. "You should come with us to Jed's for the next meeting."

"I thought that was for vets. I don't have PTSD."

"Seems like you do." Luke's warm voice was knowing as he wrapped an arm around my shoulders and kissed my temple. "You can come home with me. There's plenty of room."

"No thanks. I don't want to put you out."

"You won't put me out."

I gave him a pointed look. "Okay then, I don't want Lily to think I'm a baby."

"She won't think you're a baby."

"Allow me to rephrase. I'm all freaked out right now, but it's already going away. I don't want her to *treat* me like a baby."

"Oh, well that changes things then." He laughed. "She'll baby the shit out of you."

Liam laughed too. "Yeah, she will, but that's a good thing. She wants everybody to be happy. That's all she cares about."

"I know that, and I love it. But I want to be a grown up about this."

"Then I'll stay with you," Liam offered. "I'll sleep right here on the couch."

"What about Cheddar?"

"He's having a sleepover with Dylan tonight." He let out an exaggerated sigh. "I might end up losing custody of my cat to him. They are now best friends."

That made my messed-up insides feel gooey in a good way. "Aww, that's just the cutest mental image ever."

"I know, it's adorable. And listen, we have to talk, but it can wait until morning, okay?"

"Okay. Talk in the morning," I repeated. "Why are you guys here anyway? How did you know? I mean—"

"All the lights are on. From up the road, the place looked as bright as Times Square," Luke answered. "So we stopped to check on you. You didn't answer your phone or the door, so here we are."

"I've been having a rough time, as you know," Liam added. "I spent the day with Luke, and we were jogging me into exhaustion so I could go home and crash."

"Cade was here earlier today. I probably should have asked him to stay." Dejected and exhausted, I flopped back on the chaise part of the sectional and yanked the quilt over my head to hide. Rocky hopped up next to me, letting out a whine as he bumped the side of my face with his nose. "This is humiliating."

I felt the chaise dip as Liam sat at my side. "Give yourself some grace, Holly," he whispered as he pulled the quilt from my face then cupped my cheek in his big, warm palm.

"Ha. Touché," I mumbled. Grace left the building once I'd started freaking out.

"I'm going to head back home," Luke stood. "Love you, Holls. Come on, Rocky."

"Love you too. I'd say don't tell Lily about this, but secrets haven't exactly been working out for me lately."

"Try to get some sleep you two. I'll lock up."

I waited until Luke and Rocky were out of earshot, but I had to ask. "Are we okay?"

"Yes. Well, we will be, but don't worry about that right now. If you're tired, get some sleep and we'll talk in the morning."

"I'll sleep right here. You take my bed. You'll be more comfortable."

"You sure?"

"Yes, I'm about to crash anyway. Moving will only wake me up."

"All right." He leaned forward to place a kiss on my forehead. "Goodnight, sunshine."

Sunshine.

I smiled as he walked away.

He was back.

With a sigh of relief, I drifted off to sleep.

I awoke what had to be hours later to a crash from upstairs.

Groggy, I threw off the quilt and headed up the spiral staircase to check on Liam.

I found him shivering in the dark. He'd kicked the covers halfway off the bed and it looked like he'd flung his arm out in his sleep and knocked the side table over. I righted it and replaced the lamp.

The part of the covers still on the bed rode low over

his hips. He was half on his stomach and half on his side with one of his legs drawn up. I could see the deep V of his abs and the side of his muscular hip, and I gasped on a sharply inhaled breath when I realized he was nude. Moonlight shone over his bare skin, casting him in silver shadows. He was beautiful, and I wanted to be in that bed with him more than anything.

He trembled and moaned softly as he tossed to his side, and I felt my heart crack wide open as I watched him struggle.

I pulled the quilt up to his waist then gently placed a hand on his shoulder. "Liam," I whispered gently. A squeal escaped when he swept me into the bed, and I ended up pinned halfway beneath his big warm body. Then I positively melted when he hugged me tight like a human body pillow and laid his head on my chest.

"It's dark," he mumbled into my neck. "Turn the light on, sunshine."

"No, it's okay like this." I relaxed, letting myself settle into the pillows. "Go back to sleep."

"But you don't like the dark." Sleepy eyes met mine and my heart turned over in my chest at the tenderness I saw in his gaze.

"I know," I whispered. "But I like you."

"Stay with me?" The thread of vulnerability I heard in his voice almost broke me and all I wanted was for him to finally get some rest.

"Yes, baby, I'm here," I soothed as I stroked his hair back from his face. "Go back to sleep. I promise I won't go anywhere."

Like I could go anywhere pinned halfway beneath him like I was. And why would I want to be anywhere else but right here? I'd been fantasizing about being with him like this for months.

He squeezed me tight, sliding a leg between mine and snuggling his head between my breasts before I felt him finally relax as he fell back to sleep.

The rugged strength in his features had softened. He was gorgeous. I watched him while an array of expressions crossed his face as he dreamed. His jaw clenched, his eyebrows drew down, and his arms tightened around me as a shudder shot through his body. A hot ache grew in my throat and tears filled my eyes. I wished I could join him in his sleep and chase the nightmares away.

With a light caress, I stroked his jaw until it unclenched then worked my way down over his broad shoulders and upper back until he sighed against my chest and relaxed into peaceful dreams again.

"Holly . . ." he mumbled.

"Shh, you're okay." I smoothed his hair and kissed the top of his head, pleased when he relaxed even more until he was practically limp in my arms.

I watched him sleep until I couldn't keep my eyes open anymore.

Sunbeams surrounded us when I woke up hours later. They sparkled through the paned windows to create our own golden little world up here, like we'd woken up inside of a sunny, yellow kaleidoscope. I felt just like I remembered when I was a kid, peaceful and serene, but it was so much better now that I had Liam by my side to share it with.

"Wake up, sleepyhead. Look at all that sunshine coming through the windows." I nudged him awake, feeling him stretch against me as his eyes fluttered open. "It's magic up here in the morning. Baby, look."

"I don't need to look out the window. You're all the sunshine I need. You lit my way out of the dark last night, didn't you?"

I inhaled a sharp breath at the beauty of his words. "Well, you made me brave again. I stayed in the dark with you and actually fell asleep in it. Maybe the moonlight is magic up here too."

"Look at us, making progress." His body rumbled with sleepy laughter. I loved the sound of his laugh but feeling it against me was the best.

"I would have destroyed this if we hadn't become friends first," I confessed on a whispered sigh.

He nodded, tickling my neck with his hair. "I wasn't ready for you when we first met." His eyes shifted up to catch mine in his smiling gaze. "But I am now. And I swear, I'll never doubt what we have again."

"I swear it too. This is real. What we have is too special to ever put at risk with irrational fears and stupid doubts." I squeezed him tight. "We're past that now, I know we are."

I didn't like the sorrow on his face as he looked up at me. "I hate what I said to you and I'm so sorry for leaving you alone like I did."

"Please don't be. I understand."

Earnest eyes met mine. "When we started out, I was too busy building armor, protecting myself, thinking all the wrong things. Instead of wondering how I would inevitably hurt you, how I would fail you when I eventually broke, I should have been asking myself what I still had left inside of me to give to you. How I could make you happy. I make you happy, don't I?" His voice dropped low as he asked for reassurance.

"Yes, so much. I've never felt anything close to the way you make me feel. And you don't need armor, Liam." I cupped his face in my palms. "Not when you are already fucking unbreakable. I would never hurt you, not ever. I would die first. I—I love you, Liam."

He pulled me lower on the bed and deeper into his arms, so we were eye to eye. Then he pulled me tight, so we were pressed close, heart to heart. "And I'm in love with you, Holly. From the moment I saw you, I knew it. You changed everything for me, and I'll never let you go."

Chapter 19
Liam

She was mine. There was no going back for us now. Her big blue eyes glittered in the early morning sunrise, brimming with tenderness and promises as she held my face in her soft warm palms and kissed me.

"You're the one for me and I'm going nowhere. I promise you that, Liam."

I could only hope to find the right words to express how full my heart felt right now. "I've waited for this moment, wished for it, dreamed of it every fucking night since I met you. I never want this to end. I've wanted you for so damn long." I sealed my lips to hers, thrusting my tongue into her mouth, desperate to get as close to her as I possibly could.

Pulling away to catch her breath, she said, "This doesn't have to end, Liam. We have all the time in the world." She ran the backs of her fingertips down my face then kissed me sweet. "Oh, before we start, I went to the store." Her lips moved against mine as she spoke. "The bedside table is full of every kind of condom you can imagine. I know it's not our Friday, but we don't need to wait anymore."

It was inevitable now, me and her. This was going to happen, and I almost couldn't take it. "No more waiting."

"No more waiting," she repeated. "I want every part of you to be mine, Liam. Everything." She was greedy-eyed and flushed in the cheeks, and more fucking beautiful than anything I'd ever seen.

I nodded. I'd give her anything she asked for and I'd die doing it if I had to.

I had never felt like this before.

Overpowered.

Overwhelmed.

I was in over my head with this woman, and I never wanted to come back up. I would rather drown in her depths than ever breathe on my own again.

"This is almost too much for me, Holly. The way I feel for you." I had to tell her. She had to know what she did to me. The power she held over my heart.

"I feel it too. You're it for me, Liam." her voice was nothing but a wisp of air between us, but the meaning of her words gave me strength. "And you never have to worry again because I'm yours, remember?"

"I need you naked. Right now. I have to feel you."

"Yes. Oh god, let's make this real, Liam."

She wore a thin cotton nightgown, and I wanted it gone. I tugged on the hem, and she lifted her body so I could pull it over her head as she reached down to shimmy out of her panties.

Skin against skin, we melted into each other. I kissed her and all the pent-up longing I'd held in my heart exploded as her tongue slid against mine and she whimpered into my mouth.

I was hard and she was nothing but soft, wet perfection as she threw her leg over my hips and I pressed myself against her, shoving her to her back to tease her entrance with the head of my cock. I couldn't hold back anymore, not when it felt like I was falling apart at the seams as my love for her overwhelmed me.

I was coming undone, and we hadn't even gotten started. It took all the strength inside me not to just shove inside and take her hard. To pound into her until everything else faded and it was just me and her, bodies and souls intertwined like they were meant to be from the day we met.

But I had planned to be gentle our first time together. I wanted to love her like she deserved, not fuck her into the crazed oblivion my body was driving me toward at the mere thought of finally getting inside that sweet little body of hers.

With a grunt, I slid down, trailing my lips over her soft skin as I nipped at her neck, then moved lower to take a nipple into my mouth with a soft pull.

"I want you now," she whispered, threading her fingers into my hair to tug me back up. She let me go and reached to the side to open the drawer of the bedside table.

I sat up on my knees and grabbed a box, tearing it open to pull out a strip of condoms. I sheathed myself then slid a hand up the inside of her thigh, watching her shiver as I reached the top. I stroked her opening with my thumb, slipping it inside to find her wet and ready for me. I pulled my thumb out and circled her clit, and when her breath hitched I looked up at her face to find eyes blazing with need. I dropped forward, covering her body with mine as I balanced above her with my forearms planted firmly in the bed.

Her breath came in hitching little gasps as I entered her. Her legs spread wide and she bent her knees to press them into my sides.

I braced myself over her, prepared to stop at any moment. "Am I hurting you? I know I'm big. I'll go slow." I eased back out.

"No. I want all of you. Right now. Every inch of you could be inside me and I'd still want you closer. Don't you dare stop." She grabbed my ass and pulled me in, thrusting her hips up to meet mine.

We fit together like she was made for me.

I thrust in and out, slow and smooth, but ending with a hard press so I could grind against her clit.

"How are you like this?" she breathed.

I groaned into her neck as I licked and sucked at the soft skin of her throat. "Like what?"

"So gentle, but also rough at the same time. I love how you make me feel. Like you cherish me."

I sank deep and met her eyes. "I do." It was as simple as that. "I love you."

"I love you too."

She tightened around me, so I gave her more, sliding a hand between our bodies to rub circles around her clitoris as I kissed her deep.

"Faster, Liam. I need you." She wound her legs around my back and threw her arms up to grab hold of the headboard.

Our eyes met again and held as I drove into her. Taking her like I wanted.

Hard.

Fast.

Out of control.

I shifted up to my knees and held her open with my hands digging into the inside of her spread thighs. My hips slammed into hers and she cried out my name, urging me on and telling me I better not dare fucking stop.

"Please," she mewled as I ground my pelvis into hers, rocking us both into a blind frenzy of pleasure.

I'd never felt like this. She'd unlocked something in me. My soul jolted and my heart pounded in my chest, the beat matching my wild thrusts into her body. Everything was in sync as I made her mine. This was meant to be.

"Liam, Liam, Liam . . ." She repeated my name in an ever-increasing tempo as she moved closer to release. I felt her shudder beneath me, her thighs tightening and her back arching off the bed as her head shifted to the side and her eye slammed shut.

"Look at me," I demanded, pushing my thumb

against her clit. Her eyes met mine as waves of pleasure radiated outward from the base of my spine. "I want to watch you come." I was almost there but she had to go first.

"I'm so close." She let go of the headboard and reached for me. "Kiss me."

Our tongues tangled in time with the rhythm we'd found together as she pulled me tight, winding her arms around my neck as I drove into her once, twice, before we went over the edge together.

Gathering her in my arms, I rolled to my side with her head on my chest. I stroked her hair out of her face and kissed the top of her head.

"That was unbelievable," she whispered as she shivered in my arms.

"And we can do it again and again. Whenever you want me, I'm yours." I kissed her, then discreetly turned to remove the condom and wrap it in a tissue from the box on the table to get rid of later.

I sucked in a breath as she fit herself along my back. Arm around my waist, soft tits pressed between my shoulder blades as she kissed a trail along the scar that wound across my upper back. "I'm yours too," she whispered.

"Damn, Holly. I knew I'd never get enough. I'm already hard for you again. Only you could do this to me."

"Poor baby. I'd say I was sorry, but I'm not. I'll move over here." She scooted over, putting space between us. I turned to my other side, where I could now see all of her;

the deep curve of her waist, her full, rosy-tipped breasts, and all that gorgeous blonde hair flowing over her shoulder. The sight only made me get harder.

I sat up against the headboard and raised an eyebrow, wrapping my fist around my cock with a sardonic shake of my head.

She tilted her head to the bedside table with a grin. I found another condom and rolled it on.

She sat up and still trembling from her orgasm, threw her leg over my hips to straddle my cock. We both gasped as the tip entered her.

With her head thrown back, long hair brushing my thighs, and her gorgeous tits reddened from my mouth and beard, she was exquisite. I watched her pussy stretch wide as inch by slow inch she took me inside again. Her inner muscles fluttered and squeezed on the descent and it drove me wild. When her hips met mine, I slammed my eyes shut with a desperate growl. I wanted this to last.

"I love the way you feel inside me. Like you belong right here." She rode me slowly, languidly, taking her time to build us both up again.

I opened my eyes to see her running her hands up and down her body, tweaking the tight tip of a nipple with one hand and sliding the other low to part her fingers around my cock, gripping it tight each time she rose over me. "Do you want to come again, Liam?" she whispered on a moan.

"Fuck. Yes," I ground out through the tight clench of my jaw. My body was strung tight with the need for it. I was about to explode.

"I'm almost there again, baby. Let yourself go."

I had no idea she would be this sexy. She was like a siren out of a myth, or a witch weaving a spell. I was hers.

She threw her head back and her hands hit my thighs behind her as she came again. The sight of her bared to me, spread apart on my cock as she tightened and pulsed, pushed me over too and I yanked her into my arms, wrapping myself around her as I shuddered with my release.

"I love you so fucking much," I groaned into her neck.

Wrapping me in her arms, she whispered, "I love you too."

Chapter 20
Holly

Liam and I had become inseparable. We'd spent the next few days working together on the store and preparing for the Street Festival. Shelves, counter space, and display tables for the main part of the shop were in place and ready to be filled with the inventory I'd been busy creating. My garden was thriving and well on its way to becoming the lush backyard paradise I used to love when Gram and Grandpa had run this place.

We had spent our nights making love and talking at his place so we could take care of Cheddar. We shared secrets and got to know each other even better. But there was still one thing I hadn't told him—the one thing that prevented me from being fully at peace here.

We were having coffee in my garden. The smell of lavender and rosemary scented the air as we sat at the white iron table I'd placed beneath the arched trellis Liam had repaired.

"I need to tell you what happened before I came back to Sweetbriar."

His eyes snapped to mine, and he set his cup down. "Are you sure? There's no pressure to tell me, Holly. I want you to know that. Even if you never tell me, it will be okay. It's not a secret I have to know. As long as you feel safe, nothing else matters."

I loved how protected and cared for he made me feel. "I'm ready. I have to do this. It's the one thing preventing me from feeling like I'm completely at home. Like a secret that everyone only sort of knows about and it's haunting me. Do you know how that feels? I have to let it go. I need to get it out."

I nodded. "I know exactly how that feels."

"I had a feeling that you would." I exhaled, looking around the yard. It was peaceful. I was safe. That night in the tent felt like it happened in another lifetime.

He reached for my hand, tugging until I stood up so he could pull me sideways into his lap and deep into the circle of his arms. I rested my head on his chest and Liam propped his feet up on the chair I had been sitting in. "Now you can tell me," he murmured. Now that I was surrounded by his warmth and as safe as I could ever hope to be.

"You seem to always know what I need. How did I get so lucky?"

He squeezed me tight. "We're both lucky."

"I put a man into a coma, Liam."

His sharp intake of breath was the only response he gave.

"I was asleep in my tent. Hiking a trail I'd been on enough times that I felt comfortable there. He cut through the side with a knife then held it to my throat."

"Sunshine . . ." He breathed as his arms tightened around me. He knew not to react. He'd been through enough himself and had enough therapy to know that listening was what I needed him to do.

"I fought. Got the knife away from him. Then I shoved him off me and tackled him hard. He hit his head on a rock when he fell. It knocked him unconscious, and it took days before he woke up. I wasn't the only one he attacked that night, but I was the last. They said I won't have to testify. There's enough evidence to put him away for a long time without my help. But even though it's been over for months it wouldn't stop haunting me until now. I talked to the cops after it happened. A therapist. My dad. Cade. But I couldn't get all of it out of me until right now with you."

After a few minutes spent holding me tight and stroking my hair, he said, "I'm proud of you." He ducked his head to look me in the eyes. "You're a strong woman, Holly."

"Thank you. And I know it will never fully let me go —things like that never truly go away. Just, in this moment right now, with you, it's not here."

"I feel that all the time when I'm with you." I tipped my head back to see his face as he spoke. "You give me peace."

I smiled. "I'm glad I told you. Now there's nothing between us."

His lips met mine. And I turned in his lap so I could put my arms around him and hold him back.

We sat there in the sun, letting the moment settle into our hearts as we felt the peace we had discovered in each other soothe us.

Finally, Liam broke the silence. "Big day tomorrow."

"Rosemary's Apothecary makes its debut at the Sweetbriar Street Festival tomorrow. I can hardly believe it."

"I can. You're amazing."

I bumped him with my shoulder. "I could say the same about you."

"I think we should move in together," he suggested, his fingers drifting lightly along my spine.

"Here? We can pack up Cheddar and your stuff and make everything official after the grand opening. It will give us time to get everything ready."

"I love that idea."

"Good. Now I have to tell you something." I winced.

"Uh-oh. That sounds a bit ominous . . ."

I took a deep breath. "Gram and I are riding with Jared to the festival in the morning."

His body tightened beneath me. "Why?"

"Uh, please don't freak out. I have zero proof of this, only a gut feeling. Jared has always had a crush on me, ever since we were kids. I have this weird feeling he's planning on jerking me around with the permits for my store if I don't play nice with him."

"Oh, well you have nothing to worry about. Call him and cancel. Luke texted me earlier. Everything is done.

Permits have been processed, approved, and filed. Rosemary's Apothecary is good to go."

I whipped out my phone and texted Jared immediately to cancel. "Yay!"

Liam huffed out a deep sigh. "I do not like that guy."

"I don't either. Never have." I grinned up at him with relief flooding through my system.

He kissed me and the relief was soon replaced with heat.

"Let's go inside," he growled against my lips. "Let me take your mind off everything." His hand slid between my legs, stroking gently as he whispered how much he loved me in my ear.

"Why? You can do whatever you want to me right here. Isn't it beautiful out here with the sun finally coming out to shine?"

"Not as beautiful as you are."

We spent the rest of the day making love in my garden on a quilt in the grass and whispering our plans for the future.

Chapter 21
Holly

I hadn't been to a Sweetbriar festival since I left town, but I used to enjoy them as a kid. The Sweetbriar Street Festival was fairly new, but from what I could tell as I peered out the front window of Vi's shop, it was a typical example of how overboard this town went when it came to celebrating itself.

Main street was blocked off from end to end with traffic being rerouted through a few of the side roads. The town's center courtyard was already decorated with balloons and banners while all the community buildings that surrounded it—the library, city hall, police and fire station—had their doors open to visitors with representatives stationed outside to greet them. People were already gathering in the courtyard to wait for the festival to officially begin and I was gradually becoming overwhelmed.

Liam had helped me put together my display. I didn't need a booth, as I was lucky enough to score the spot directly in front of Violet's shop. She let me move the tables and chairs out of the covered patio area adjacent to the front door. We set up two long tables in an L shape. I had mini free samples as well as an array of things to sell. If my store was a success, I'd eventually have to hire help to make my products, but for now I was sticking to a very small-scale collection and stuff I would make to order.

My eyes bugged out as I watched people setting up their booths. There was even a stage set up at one end of the street with a wooden dance floor in front. Various local bands were scheduled to play throughout the day.

A surge of panic shot through me.

What had I been thinking?

How was I supposed to fit in with all these experienced business owners when I had no idea what I was doing?

I huffed out a big breath and said, "Sheesh, this is going to be huge. This is way more than I expected."

"It's a big deal," Violet remarked as she joined me at the window. "I get swamped all day long every year. Having your booth right out front is going to be amazing for you."

Her shop was in a log cabin themed shopping center across the street from the community courtyard where all the city buildings were located.

"This is too much. Am I really ready for this type of event? My store isn't even open yet—"

She pulled me in for a quick hug then wrapped her arm around my shoulders as we watched what was happening out the window together. "First of all, you'll be fine. All my baristas will be here today so I can pop outside and help you whenever you need it. And second, this will be a huge boost for your business. Everyone in town will get a chance to see what you have to offer." She scoffed. "I hate to say it, but Jared was right about that. Where is he, anyway? I expected him to be glued to your side all day like the pesky little dipshit he's shown himself to be."

I let out a soft laugh. "He's busy escorting Gram around."

"Oh boy, and probably being subjected to a few of her colorful stories too, am I right?"

"Well, since she referred to him as her 'good lookin' beck-and-call boy' when he ran into us this morning, I'd say yes. Mental torture is definitely on her agenda for the day."

"God bless that woman. Hopefully it works so you don't have to take care of him yourself. I get how awkward it has been for you. Probably annoying as hell, too."

"You could say that, but it's over now. According to Luke, every permit has been approved and is now on file. Rosemary's Apothecary is ready for the grand opening next week. All the ducks are in a row and there is nothing Jared can do about it now, not unless he wants to look like a huge unprofessional asshole. Mom is friends with his mother, but she doesn't expect me to tolerate his shit on her behalf." I shrugged, no longer concerned. "So, I'm done with him. Today is his last chance to act like a normal human being and be my friend. If he chooses to keep being a chauvinistic pest, then I'll handle it." I wanted to be an adult about this. I wanted him to fade away and leave me alone. He was not a good person, and I wanted him out of my life with no conflict or drama. But I had the feeling that was probably too much to wish for.

"Good for you. Oh, here comes Liam with your banner and fliers!" Luke's office was across the parking lot from Violet's shop. McCabe Construction had a table set up out front of their building, but since Lily was due to give birth this month, Luke would not be leaving her side. They were officially on baby watch, so Liam would represent the business today and handle anything that came up until Luke went back to work.

"Rosemary's Apothecary is official now. Once that banner goes up, there's no going back. I can do this. Can't I?" I tried and failed to keep the slightly panicked tone out of my voice.

"Hell yes you can. You're already doing it, and I'm so proud of you."

Her reassurance meant the world to me. I took a steadying breath. "I'm doing this," I repeated. A small grin slid across my face. "I still can't believe it."

"Well believe it, girl. Liam is about to string up your banner. Don't look until Gram gets here, she wants you to see it together for the first time. I'll text her to ditch that weenie, Jared, and get over here."

"I can't wait." I headed for the sofa in the corner to wait.

"Where's your grandma?" Liam asked as he headed my way with a grin bright enough to light up the entire town. God, he was gorgeous. And hot, and kind, and good with hands, and his dick, and his mouth, and everything he'd ever done, or will do in the future.

Damn, I had it bad.

After coming to my senses, I held up my arms. "Vi's texting her. Come sit with me."

He plopped in the corner of the couch and slid his arm across the back, gesturing with his finger for me to go to him, so I did. *Duh.*

I snuggled into his side as he wrapped me up in those big arms of his. "We should sneak into the back room," he whispered in my ear. "Take a Chance Day is pretty soon. No Pants Day is coming up fast too. We don't have any balloons or mistletoe, but we could kiss the hell out of each other anyway."

"And recreate our accidental Valentine's Day kiss?"

"Except this time, I can do all the things I couldn't before," he whispered in my ear.

I liked the sound of that. "Like what?"

"Like slide my hand up your dress and make you come against the door." His breath tickled my neck as he whispered in my ear.

"I want that, so bad. But we'll have to be fast so we don't get caught. It's going to be busy here very soon."

His eyes darkened. Had he expected me to say no to this absolutely genius idea?

Wordlessly we stood and he grabbed my hand. I followed him across the shop, through the swinging doors and into the hall. He opened the door to the storage area and yanked me through. I kicked it closed and he shoved me against it, caging me in with his strong arms.

"Maybe I should go down on you instead." His voice was like gravel, nothing but dark, sexy growly grit. The muscles in his jaw ticked as he stared down at me with heat blazing in his eyes. "It'd be faster."

I tilted my head to the side. "Aww, this will be our first time for that."

A slight smile ghosted across his face, but he didn't answer. He seemed determined so I lost the sentimentality and got down to business.

"Okay." I nodded decisively. "But listen, getting caught back here with your head shoved between my legs will not be the same as getting busted making out."

"Two minutes. That's all I need." He cupped me between my legs with a wicked grin.

"Awfully sure of yourself, aren't you?" I shuddered as his fingers pressed against my already aching center.

He leaned in and slid his nose up my neck to whisper in my ear. "You're already wet for me, and I haven't even kissed you yet."

I threw my arms around his neck. "Like I told you last night. You do things to me, Liam."

"I'm about to do a few things to you. That Valentine's Day kiss we shared has haunted my dreams ever since it happened, Holly. It's going to be so much better this time around."

He dropped to his knees and slid his hands up my legs, pushing my dress up on the way. He ducked beneath and pulled my undies down. I stepped out of them, and he shoved them into his back pocket.

I shivered, suddenly acutely aware that this could end up being an extremely bad idea if we got caught. "Oh god. Hurry." I mean, I was leaning against the door to the shop and the back door was locked. The odds were in our favor that we wouldn't get busted, but still . . .

"Put your leg over my shoulder and hold on," he ordered.

I did what he said and not even a second later he bit the inside of my thigh, then licked his way straight up my center to my clit, pulling it into his mouth with a powerful, and dare I say, *confident* swirl of his tongue.

"Good lord, Liam." My hands immediately went to his head to hold him close. I yanked my dress up then tunneled my fingers in his hair, pulling it tight as I shoved myself against his mouth and rolled my hips.

He knew what he was doing, and he wasted no time. He held my ass tight in his hands, digging into my flesh as he went at me with his tongue. Then two of his fingers slid inside me from behind and I almost cried out. Somehow, I managed to keep quiet.

"You're great at this," I panted. "Pretty sure I'm gonna need it every day now."

My legs began to shake. He looked up at me with his gorgeous, smoldering brown eyes and let out a muffled laugh. His lips slid against my slick skin as he found my clit again, and I let out a whimper. He was smug AF down there and I couldn't blame him.

I tried to decide if I should be embarrassed at how fast he was about to get me off or not. I decided on *not*, because what could possibly be bad about coming all over his face? There was no way for me to lose in this situation.

"Faster," I demanded, and he sucked me faster. "More." He added a third finger and went deeper, thrusting hard to find that exact spot inside that pushed me right up to the edge, then over it. "Oh my, oh god, Liammmm," I hissed as I went *off*. Sparks flew as my vision shimmered white around the edges and I almost fell over.

He replaced his mouth with a gentle hand, stroking me gently as he stood up to band an arm around my waist. "If sunshine had a taste, it would be this pussy," he growled in my ear.

After a few seconds of blissed out silence while I collected myself, caught my breath, and regained my footing, I answered. "I had no idea you were so filthy, Liam." I panted as I stood there trembling in his arms.

He didn't answer. However, the grinding thrust of his erection into my stomach said it all.

"All that sweetness and good manners covered up a lot, huh? Like, you literally made me come in less than two minutes. *I* can't even make me come in less than two minutes. I need at least five and a fully charged friend. You have a gift. One that I'm determined to exploit every day for the rest of ever. God, I'm sorry I talk so much."

He shrugged with a grin, then buried his face in my neck. His beard was wet against my skin, and I wished we could go home and spend the rest of the day in bed together.

He licked up my neck to my ear to whisper, "I'm going to think about this for the rest of the day. How pretty and pink you are, how tight. The way you tasted and how wet you got for me. I can't fucking wait to get inside you again." His thumb pressed against my clit before he gave it a little pinch. "Be ready for me when we get home."

Holy shit.

"But I'm ready for you *now*," I whined. "Waiting is not my favorite. That's something you should know about me. Let's go into the bathroom. We can be fast."

He took a step back, hands at my waist. "The festival is about to start."

I whimpered out, "I don't care anymore. All I want is you."

"You'll have me, baby, and I'll give you all you can take—later."

"Damn it." I stomped my foot like a bratty kid, pulling back to shove my finger in his chest. "You're mean."

"Didn't I just get you off in under two minutes?" His answering laugh was adorably smug. "Your legs are still shaking from it, and you already want more. You're a greedy little thing, aren't you?" His teasing voice lit me up. He was right; he made me greedy, and needy, and fricking desperate to get him inside me again and I didn't care where. Maybe I should get down on my knees, suck him off, and drive him just as crazy as I felt right now.

"Mean." I pouted. "Okay, fine, you're not mean, you're very generous and I appreciate your special skills. Thinking about your dick has made me completely irrational and I'm sorry."

"Yoo hoo! Hollyberry!" It was Gram.

Liam smugly handed me my panties and I slid into them. "Damn it, Liam. You're the one who'd better get ready. Your place or mine? Once we step through whatever door we're going through, I'm going to be all over you."

"My place. I have to feed Cheddar. Go talk to your grandma, sunshine. I should probably wash up before I head out there." He ran a hand over his beard and winked at me. *Gah!*

"Coming, Gram," I shouted brightly as Liam headed for the bathroom.

"Oh, you're all rumpled," Gram observed with a sly grin. "Straighten your hair, sugar pie, and untuck your dress from your underwear," she hissed. "That should be the first thing you check. Always."

"Oh, crap, Gram. It's not what you think—"

Liam came striding out of the back room at the precise moment the lie shot out of my mouth, he untucked my dress from my panties, then dropped a kiss to my forehead as he passed us on his way to the counter.

"Uh-huh, sure. This is exactly what I think it is, honey, and good for you. Don't forget who you're talking to."

"Okay, fine. Liam and I are together. But we are

never talking about this." I circled my finger around with my eyebrows up and she nodded.

"Agreed. What you get up to with your new hunk is your business. My goodness, I can't tell you the number of times your grandpa and I almost got caught when we were up to no good together. Youth is wasted on the young." She let out a nostalgic sigh. "Anyhoo, let's get outside, it's about to start." She grabbed both my hands and gave them a squeeze. "Our first Sweetbriar Street Festival."

I squeezed back. "It's official. Rosemary's Apothecary is open for business."

"Come on. You have to see the gorgeous banner. The permanent version will be on the store next week, just in time for opening day, and I can't wait." We crossed the shop and went out the front door. Violet waved to us from behind the counter on our way with a huge grin on her face.

We made it through the door, and I froze.

The banner said *Holly's Apothecary*. Beautiful gold letters on a deep green background.

My name.

"Gram?" I murmured as Liam came up from behind to wrap me in a big bear hug and kiss my neck.

Gram beamed up at me. "Ultimately, it's your store, honey. You've done all the hard work and you'll be the one to run it and keep it going. I was just along for the ride. I figured it's only right that it has your name. Do you like it?"

Tears filled my eyes as Liam kissed my cheek then let

me go so I could maniacally flail my arms and lose my shit without causing him injury. "I love it, Gram. But most of all, I love you and all the faith you have in me. I will make you proud, I swear."

"You already make me proud, sweetheart, and you always have. So, so proud."

She pulled me into a hug, and I kissed the top of her head. "This is going to be amazing."

Today would be a whirlwind, I could tell already. Between the fabulous O from Liam that had just wrecked me to the high from Gram naming the store after me, I don't think I'd ever been this full of joy. I swung around for another look at the banner, then took in the tables full of my products, eyeing all of the things I had made with my own two hands. Tears filled my eyes.

I did that. *Me.*

How was it possible to be this happy?

My head had shot straight up to the clouds. I felt like running around Vi's patio in a blissed-out zoomie circle like Cheddar was so fond of doing. However, I refrained and managed to keep up the pretense of being an adult—barely.

"There you are!" Jared waved as he crossed the parking lot toward me. "I've been looking all over for you, sweetie. You're stunning in that dress. So lovely." His eyes raked up and down as he reached for my hand. I shook it briefly before taking a step back.

Well shit.

Down to earth again.

Jared's approach had proved that one hundred

percent contentment was simply not possible. I would have to deal with him once and for all. He was clearly not ready to give up on whatever he thought we would be doing today.

"Rosemary," he greeted Gram. "I couldn't find anyone selling funnel cakes. I'm so sorry. How are your feet?"

She immediately sat in one of the chairs we'd left for us to sit in if things got slow, her eyes shifting to the side as she innocently shrugged. "I could swear that I heard someone mention funnel cakes."

Liam's possessive hands slid around my waist from behind before settling on my hips in an unmistakably clear declaration of *mine*.

This should be interesting.

"She's been here with me all morning," Liam informed him. "What do you need?"

"Uh, nothing. I was going to introduce her to—um, a few people."

I twisted in Liam's arms. The expression on his face would have scared me if he weren't using it on my behalf. My goodness, mean and threatening really were his specialties.

I turned back to watch Jared blanch and take a step back.

"Bring whoever it is over here," I diplomatically suggested. "I appreciate how generous you are, Jared. It's so kind of you to want to help me get things off the ground. You've always been a good friend to me."

"Yeah, of course." His answering smile was dull; it

didn't reach his eyes, and it gave me a chill. I watched, shivering as he turned and walked away.

I stepped into the warmth of Liam's body, thankful he was still standing at my back. He slid his arms around me, crossing them as he enveloped me in the steady, solid strength of his embrace. "I don't like how he looks at you," he murmured. "I have to head over to Luke's table, but I want you to stay in my sight all day. Do not go anywhere with him. Stay on this patio, okay? Don't even go into the shop without me. I have a bad feeling about him. I just can't put my finger on it yet."

Nodding, I agreed. "I'll stay right here unless I'm with you. I promise."

"Good girl. Thank you. I'll feel better if I can keep an eye you." He dropped a kiss to the top of my head. "Later, Rosemary."

"Oh my." Gram's eyebrows shot up. "You really are something else, Liam. Let the record show I was right about you. I'll keep my eye on our Holly. If he comes back, I'll make sure he doesn't get any wise ideas. I can be a real pain in the ass when I need to be."

True to my word, I stayed right here the entire time. And thankfully, Jared did not come back.

Chapter 22
Liam

We decided to meet Holly's family for dinner at Holloway's before going back to my place. The day had gone by in a blur of activity and noise, and I was so glad it was over. She sold everything at her table like I knew she would, and I couldn't be happier for her. She had no idea how amazing she was, and I was determined to show her every day how much she meant to me.

"Are you doing okay? You're pretty quiet over there." She sat silent and still in the passenger seat of my truck with her head leaning against the window. "Taking it all in?"

"Yeah." She lifted her head and grinned at me. "I can't believe how great today went. I sold everything. All of it. And I have so many custom orders for more. I might have to hire someone to work with me right off the bat. I broke even and then some. I can't believe it. I think I might end up being good at this, Liam."

"Of course you will." I slid my hand up her leg, giving it a squeeze for emphasis. "You're going to kick some apothecary store ass."

Shy laughter filled the cab of my truck then she took my hand and kissed it. "Gosh, I hope so. But right now all I care about is food. I'm starving."

"We're almost there." Headlights flashed in my review mirror, and I frowned. Someone was following too close for comfort.

"I can't stand tailgaters," she muttered.

I swung into Holloway's parking lot, dismayed when the tailgater followed me in and parked next to me. "Great. Stay inside," I instructed after I parked. "I'll handle this."

"No, let's just go home and call Cade or my dad. I don't want you getting into a fight or something—wait a second. Is that Ava and Maren?" She squinted into the glare of the parking lot lamp and determined that it was them. "Oh hell no, *you* stay here, and *I'll* handle this. I am in no mood for their crap right now. I want a cheeseburger and a beer, and I am not ordering the side of bullshit they are probably dishing out." Before I could stop her, she threw open her door and stomped around the truck.

The tall blonde one who was driving was already outside. She held up a hand. "We come in peace. Chill out, Holly, Okay? We missed you at the festival, so we decided to follow you here because this can't wait."

"What is it?" she barked. "I had a great day and I don't want you screwing it up for me. Oh, let me introduce you." She reached back blindly to flop a hand in my chest. "Liam, this is Ava and Maren, two of the pains in my ass over the last decade or so." She pointed to them in turn.

"Yeah, well it was mutual a decade ago, wasn't it?" Ava huffed. "But forget the past, we have a common pain in the ass in the present that needs dealing with. It has come to our attention that we have all been lied to," she announced.

"Yeah, and I have been used," Maren chimed in. Mascara ran in a black river down her face, and she swiped at it with an angry hand.

I had no idea what on earth was going on and turned to Holly to gauge her reaction. She froze as a contemplative look crossed her face. "Let me guess. This is about Jared, isn't it?"

Maren nodded. "Yep. He dumped me. He's been stringing me along for years, using me for a piece of ass, making me think he cared about me when apparently, according to Tess's sister at the Stop and Go this morning, all he has ever wanted was you."

I knew it. That weaselly piece of sh—

"Elizabeth had a lot to say when we were there earlier picking up break up supplies," Ava announced. "That girl is pretty hardcore, by the way. She lectured us clear into next week about chicks before dicks, ovaries before brovaries, and the rise of the incel in western American culture. And she also told us all the shit he's been spreading around about the two of you. Apparently, you're a man-eating, social climbing whore and Maren is a sad, desperate slut he feels sorry for."

"So, yeah," Maren interrupted. "Jared dumped me because he's obsessed with you. I think he's sick in the head. You need to watch out for him." She jerked her finger at me. "Watch her. Jared is a huge fucking asshole and I have no idea what he'll do now that he knows that we know what he's been up to. His cover as Sweetbriar's suave hottie has officially been blown."

I was unsurprised by this news. Holly was visibly horrified and said, "I'm so sorry, Maren."

"That's not important right now," Ava insisted. "Sorry, Maren, but it's not. We have things to tell you. It's one thing for us to fight with each other when we had our own reasons, you know?"

Maren threw out a hand. "But it's complete bullshit when someone lies for his own agenda. Our shit with you has been in the past for a long time. We had no problem with you anymore, and I do not appreciate being used like this." Tears filled her eyes as she choked on a sob. "I really loved him, and I thought we were about to get engaged. I'm so pissed right now."

Ava put her arm around her. "You'll be okay. Tell her. Just get it over with."

"So, it turns out none of what we thought about you was true," she addressed Holly. "He had me convinced you were trying to fuck him to get your store permits. That it was an ungodly, horrific mess in there and you were after his money and connections." She threw her arms out. "But clearly that isn't true. I saw your stuff in front of Violet's Café, and I've been following you online for years. I should have known better. But he had me riled up and ready to go after you in his defense. He kept hinting we'd get married someday." She hiccupped back a sob. "I was so fucking stupid over him."

"And he told me you were trying to get Owen back for one last time," Ava interrupted. "He said you wanted payback on me for taking him from you." She paused. "Holly, I admit that I slept with Owen when you were engaged to him and I'm so sorry. We were drunk and I didn't mean to. Honestly, I don't even remember doing it, except we woke up naked together." She took a deep breath and continued. "Anyway, look. The three of us had our beef when we were younger—well the four of us. Where has Tess been, anyway? But Maren and I have been over that for years. That was stupid kid stuff, you know? I got Owen back. We got married and I have the family I always wanted. Or at least I got what I thought I wanted. He turned out to be one huge-ass mistake. Why does he have to be so damn hot?" She heaved out a put-upon sigh.

"Once a cheater, always a cheater," Maren muttered. "I tried telling you that. Like, so many times."

"Beside the point, Maren. Damn." Ava rolled her eyes at me. "A girl can only take hearing *I told you so* so many times before she smacks a bitch, best friend or not, am I right?"

"She has a point, Maren," Holly agreed. "Be loyal."

"So, I'd apologize for the incident you had with Owen at your store but fuck him. I kicked his ass out.

He's back living with his mom and begging me to forgive him again. Not this time! Good riddance to bad rubbish is all I have to say about that. Me and the kids are staying with my parents. We'll lose the house, but it is what it is, and we'll be better off in the long run."

This situation was complete bullshit. I was tempted to find Jared and knock him out on their behalf. He needed a lesson on how to treat a woman and maybe I'd be the one to teach it. Someone sure needed to shake some sense into him. As for Ava, Luke was currently looking for a receptionist. Maybe he could hire her? After a thorough vetting, of course. Someone needed to feed all those kids of hers.

"Anyway, we feel bad." Ava swept her arm out. "Like, welcome back to Sweetbriar, Holly. Maybe we can do lunch sometime. Or go out for a drink if we can get our bar bans lifted. But, regardless if we go out or not, we're sorry.

"There's always Holloway's," I offered. "Come inside and have a drink with us? On me."

"Thanks but we can't. We're banned here too," Ava answered, and I wondered just how many fights they had gotten into in the past to get them banned from every bar in town.

"I can get this one lifted." Holly grinned, suddenly magnanimous and cheerful again, like she had two new friends to entertain. It was fucking cute. "I know the owners. If I promise them we won't wreck the place we should be good to have a drink together."

"Next time," Maren answered. "I'm still a mess. I just

want to get home so I can crawl into bed with a bottle of wine and my rage. I'm truly sorry, Holly."

"It sounds like you have nothing to apologize for. None of us do. We'll all be okay."

They exchanged numbers and promises that they'd meet sometime next week to poke over the newly uncovered information and possibly plot revenge against Jared.

"I'm sorry you had to hear all that." Holly wrapped her arms around my waist as we finally headed into Holloway's. "Past Holly was kind of a hot mess. And future Holly might end up going to prison for murdering Jared."

"No apologies. I love all the Hollys—past, present, and future. But hold off on the murder thing. I don't think conjugal visits will be enough for us. Plus, he isn't worth the effort of killing. Just ignore him and watch him fade away. Assholes like him require attention to thrive."

"Good point. And I love you too."

We entered Holloway's—finally—to a boisterous round of applause and the whole place shouting, "Surprise!" and "Congratulations!"

Holly's aunt and cousins owned Holloway's. Her uncle had opened the place decades ago; keeping it up and running had become somewhat of a family affair after he passed away. It reminded me of an Irish pub in here: long wooden bar, black and white tiled floor, family photos lining the walls. It was homey, cheerful, and the food was excellent.

Tonight was clearly meant to celebrate Holly. The green and gold *Holly's Apothecary* banner from the festival had been hung up over the bar and a huge sheet cake sat at one end next to a bouquet of yellow roses. "You guys!" she cried . . . and promptly burst into tears.

"There was no avoiding it this time," Levi announced from his spot at the bar next to Jude. "Surprise," he deadpanned.

"We're happy for you, Holls," Jude added.

She stepped into their hugs to answer. "It's okay. I'm in a much better place right now, you guys. I love this. All my favorites. Flowers, cake, family . . . Are there presents too?"

"Yes," Dahlia approached as Holly pulled away from Levi. "Your daddy and I got you this." She handed Holly a package wrapped in green paper and tied with a gold bow.

"Even your present is on theme. I want to be just like you when I grow up," Holly teased her.

"Open it," Ben, her dad, urged.

Holly tore the paper off. It was a framed photograph of her and her grandmother from earlier today, arms around each other, beneath the Holly's Apothecary banner. They stood, looking up at each other with huge smiles on their faces. It captured the essence of today perfectly. Bursting into tears, she threw herself into her mother's arms.

"I'm sorry, darling," Dahlia whispered. "I didn't see how inappropriate Jared has been with you over the years. I did a lot of thinking about it today. Can you forgive me?"

"Of course I can. Marjorie is awesome, and it must

have been hard for you to realize that your best friend's son is a useless little shit."

Dahlia squeezed her tight. "I've been wrong for a lot of years, my sweetheart. I can't help but feel it put a wedge between us, that maybe it's part of what drove you away from Sweetbriar."

Holly shook her head. "No, it wasn't. I had a severe case of wanderlust, remember? Who bought me my first camera? Who took me shopping for outdoor gear and forced me to take self-defense and outdoor safety classes before I left? That was all you and dad, and it ultimately saved my life. You've always supported my dreams when it mattered."

"Thank you for saying that. I love you, darling. Now it's time to enjoy your celebration."

"I love you too, Mom."

Her dad hugged her tight. "I'm proud of you, pumpkin."

We spotted Rosemary holding court at the rear of the bar where several tables had been pushed together for the family to sit, so we made our way over there. The place was packed to the gills with Holly's extended family, as well as the bar's customers. Music blared and people danced; it was a madhouse in here.

"Is it too crowded for you?" she stopped to ask me.

"No, it's fine. Go."

She kissed the top of Rosemary's head then stopped to hug various family members as she led me toward a relatively quiet booth in the corner.

We slid in next to each other and I let out a sigh. I

was okay; it wasn't a lie. But crowds were not my favorite thing. I much preferred to find a spot like this when I was in a crowded place, one where I could see everything happening.

"Is this better?" She asked with a soft smile. She knew what I needed, and I loved it.

"Yeah."

"We were supposed to go to your place," she leaned in and whispered in my ear as she ran a hand over my cock.

My eyes shot to hers. "We have all night, baby. You had a big day, and you need to eat something before we have an even bigger night."

"Let's make this fast. I need you." She took my hand and placed it between her legs. I bit my lip to keep from groaning out loud when I discovered she had taken off her panties at some point today. "See?"

"You're lucky there's a tablecloth to hide behind, sunshine." I let my fingers drift lightly along her slit before pulling them away with a shake of my head. "Now, if you can keep your hands to yourself like a good girl, we can do anything you want after you eat your dinner. Okay?"

"Oh really?" Her eyes lit up as she nodded with a teasing tilt to her head and leaned into my side, making sure to press her soft tits into my bicep as she did it. "Anything I want?"

"Anything," I confirmed.

Needless to say, dinner went by in a blur. All I could focus on was the fact that she was sitting next to me in a dress wearing no panties and determined to tease me into insanity about it the entire time we were here.

When we finally got back to my truck to leave, I was crazed.

"I haven't been very nice to you, have I?" She giggled. "Was I too *mean?*"

"Ahh, I see. Payback." I growled out a laugh. "Maybe I should have taken you into the bathroom before the festival. If I had bent you over the sink like you'd wanted me to, maybe I could have had dinner with your family without the mental image of what my fingers looked like buried inside you under the table torturing me the whole time." I backed the truck out of the parking spot and pulled onto the street.

"I'm sorry," she teased. "It's not about payback. It's about anticipation. I've been thinking about doing this all day. Doesn't it feel good? Knowing you're about to get everything you had on your mind during dinner?"

I glanced over at her and smiled. "Yeah, it does." She was right; my entire body hummed with anticipation. I was already hard just thinking about the possibilities of what she had in that naughty mind of hers. Holly was full of surprises—the best kind.

"Good boy." My eyes darted over to her as a smile quirked my lips up. She shot me a dirty wink as she pointed up the street. "Drive around that corner and pull over."

I did what she said, putting the truck in park but leaving the engine running.

"Slide your seat back and unzip your fly. We're about

to have another first time together and I can't wait. I'm declaring this Blow Job in My Boyfriend's Humongous Truck Day. Better get ready." Her smiling eyes met mine and my body started thrumming with pleasure before she even had a chance to put her hands on me.

I did exactly as she instructed and watched as she leaned over the console, bracing herself with her hands on either side of my thighs with her ass in the air. She slid her mouth over my cock and sucked me like she was desperate for it. And maybe she was; maybe she felt just like I did as I barreled embarrassingly fast toward an orgasm.

"Oh god," I ground out. "Your ass is in the window. Somebody could see you."

"Don't care," she mumbled as she slid me out of her mouth with a *pop*. "All I care about is making you come. Besides, hardly anyone drives down this street and your windows are tinted. That's why I picked it. Now put your hands on my head and show me how you like it."

I relaxed back in my seat as she swallowed me down. "God damn, Holly." I groaned as I slid my hands into her hair, gathering it in my palms as I gently eased her up and down. My hips rolled in an involuntary wave as she pulled away to lick up the underside and drop an open-mouthed kiss to the tip before taking me to the back of her throat again with a sexy little moan.

Her eyes smiled up at mine as she sucked me and somehow, I got the feeling the thrill of possibly being caught was a turn-on for her. Can't say I minded—not when the payoff was this good.

A shudder ran through me and heat gathered at the base of my spine in a searing bolt. I tried to pull her off before I came down her throat, but she shook her head and dug her fingers into my hips.

I let go. White hot and paralyzing, my orgasm shot through me and into her waiting mouth. "Fuck," I ground out. "Are you okay?"

She sat up smiling as she swiped her arm across her chin. Her cheeks were flushed, her lips were swollen and red, and she was stunning. "I loved that. I'm more than okay."

I stroked a hand down her face, resting my thumb against her lips before leaning over the console to kiss her. "You're so fucking beautiful like this," I whispered. I kissed the tip of her nose, then her eyes, and finally ended on her soft, sweet mouth again. "Now turn around. Knees on the seat, hands on the floor, ass up," I ordered. "It's my turn."

She didn't hesitate and neither did I. I flipped her dress up and buried my face in all that wet heat she had been torturing me with all night. I sucked her sweet little clit into my mouth and pulled hard, not stopping until her thighs shook and she was shoving her hips back into my face with rough, clumsy thrusts.

"God, Liam!"

"That's right, take what you want," I mumbled between her wild thrusts against my mouth.

"I need more, I need . . ."

I pulled back and entered her with two fingers. "Get there, sunshine." I ground the side of my other hand against her clit, bracing my forearm on the console as she rode my fingers. She rubbed herself against my hand, throwing her body back into me with hard strokes and squeezing my fingers tight like a vice. She was wild as she ruthlessly chased her pleasure, completely uninhibited, but most of all she was *mine*, and I had never been more turned on in my entire life.

She shuddered as she came apart and I grabbed her by the waist before she could fall, helping her back into the seat where she collapsed back in a sweaty, panting mess. "Did I make it up to you?" She turned to me with a sly, cat-got-the-cream smile spreading across her face.

"Yeah, baby. You did."

"Let's get out of here. I want to see Cheddar. And maybe fuck you in the shower before we go to bed. Another first time!" Joy lit her eyes then we both let out a breath when a car sped past us.

"That was too close." She laughed. "Let's go home."

A deep feeling of peace entered me as I looked into her eyes. "I like the way that word sounds coming from you. *Home*."

"You like that one? How about this one—*forever*." She took my hand and kissed the back, then held it for the entire drive back to my place.

Chapter 23
Holly

Everything since coming home to Sweetbriar had felt big—big life changes, big events, and the biggest love I could have ever imagined.

I had never been happier. At one point in my life, today would have qualified as the biggest day. But since falling in love with Liam, nothing would top the night he told me he loved me.

Today was the grand opening celebration of my store. Holly's Apothecary was officially opening its doors and I was beyond excited.

Mom and Gram helped me decorate the shop after we got it stocked full of my creations. The shelves were filled to bursting and backlit with tiny spotlights Liam had found online to surprise me with. Gauzy curtains in shades of green and yellow that Gram had embroidered with tiny flowers and herbs now graced the windows to give the place a moody glow. We went shopping at an antique store in town and purchased several crystal chandeliers which Liam had hung throughout the space. They cast everything in glittery shadows. It was serene; it was homey; it was even a little bit witchy in here.

For the grand opening, we'd decided on a classic tea party theme. Mom brought over her silver platters and tiered cake plates, and we filled them with tiny sandwiches and treats. My kitchen had been upgraded—everything was commercial quality now—and we were free to open up a tiny tea shop in the dining area beside it. We replaced the big family dining table with a few little round ones with mismatched chairs surrounding each, while black and forest green checkered tablecloths covered them. They were topped with pink peonies, while candles I had made flickered next to the flowers.

"Look at this, Holly. Just look. *You* did this. Never doubt yourself again, honey." Gram bustled in from the kitchen carrying a tray full of cookies, which now had swinging doors just like Violet's Café to keep it separated from the rest of the shop. She placed the platter on the battered dark wood buffet table we'd found at the antique store. I watched her eyes get misty as she trailed them across the shop.

"It's all us, Gram. It's time." I headed to the entrance, propping the steel door open so the pretty paned glass door in front of it closed us in. "Here goes nothing," I said and flipped the sign from "closed" to "open."

People arrived little by little throughout the day, sometimes in big groups, and sometimes one by one. Gram found a spot to knit in the seating area I had envisioned for people to relax in, which was perfect. I'd wanted her there to set that welcoming tone so people would see that they could stay awhile and not just drop in to shop. My mother was behind the cash register so I could mingle and talk to my customers. *Because I. Had. Customers.* People were buying my stuff, just like at the festival. Though it felt surreal at first, I quickly got used to it.

Today would definitely be making the top five of Holly's Best Day Ever list.

When it was nearly closing time, Liam arrived with Cheddar and a few boxes of his things and headed upstairs to unpack and get the cat settled into his new home. Tonight would be the first night of our co-habitation and I couldn't wait.

I felt like a grown up.

I felt like a professional.

And with Liam and Cheddar here I also felt a bit wifey . . . and I freaking loved it. I should really learn to cook more than meatloaf and mashed potatoes. Whatever, I had time for that. I had time for everything now that I was home, and safe, and happy, and finally dealing with my crap like an adult.

I had planted my roots deep in Sweetbriar again and I was never going to leave.

Levi and Jude showed up in time for dinner and I smiled when I realized I could take care of them for a change. "There's loads of food." I pointed toward the kitchen. "Get plates, get comfortable. Welcome to my shop!" I all but shouted at them as they laughed and headed toward the food.

My excitement was reaching the danger zone and was about to boil over.

"We'll start cleaning up and putting the food away, darling," Mom offered.

"Thank you. I need a system for this."

"You have time to figure it all out, sweetheart. Don't worry about a thing for tonight."

Jude and Levi had gone upstairs to sit with Cheddar while Liam ran out to pick up a pizza. I was about to be alone with Liam and Cheddar in our new home with a pizza and all the happiness in the world.

Then Jared showed up, striding through the door like he owned the place with a bouquet of red roses in his hand and a bottle of wine tucked beneath his arm.

"I'm here to offer my congratulations. Right before closing time, is it? Maybe we could share a toast together? To your beautiful new store."

"Oh, yeah, sorry, it's not a good time. I'm about to lock up. I'm starving and Liam is bringing a pizza,."

Levi and Jude came barreling down the stairs. "Cheddar isn't up there."

"Did Liam take him?" Jude asked.

"No. I mean, I sent you up there because I didn't want him to be alone in a new place."

"I'll keep looking." Jude ran back upstairs.

"What's happening?" Mom popped her head out of the kitchen.

"The cat is missing," Jared answered with a shrug.

"I'll go look outside." He put the flowers and wine down and headed out the front door. The strangest sense of déjà vu filtered over me as I watched him walk away.

"We'll look downstairs." Gram said. "Levi, go look in the garden just in case. He's tiny still, so he couldn't have gone far."

"Try not to worry, darling, we'll find him." Mom headed into my workroom while I frantically flipped the lights back on and scoured every corner of the shop before heading out to the front porch to look.

"Holly," Jared called out. He was down the street, close to the turnoff that led toward Luke's place. "I think he's over here. He's orange, right?"

I didn't even think; I just went running. "Yes, where is he?"

Jared didn't look right. His eyes were glassy, and his energy was off. No longer was he cool and suave; he appeared frantic and a bit desperate.

"It's my turn now, Holly, and you're going to listen to me."

"What? Where's Cheddar?" I dashed to the edge of the forest. This didn't make any sense. How could he have gotten way out here? I spun back to face Jared. "What's going on?"

"I'll tell you. But only after you listen to me first, okay?"

Every internal alarm bell I had was going wild, but I needed to know if he knew something about Cheddar. "Okay. Talk."

"It's my turn." He slapped a hand against his chest. "I

waited while you and Maren fought over that idiot you were both dating back in high school. I tried to wait for you to tire of Owen before I finally had to take matters into my own hands and push him back to Ava. But I'm losing patience again. What is happening with you and Liam? What more do I have to do to make you see you belong with me. It's my turn, damn you!" He stepped closer, and I stepped back. "I've been more than patient with you. It's time to open your eyes. God, I even convinced that idiot Owen that you wanted him back. I got him all riled up to go after you so I could step in and rescue you. What a damn joke. That Liam is always one step ahead, and I'm so tired of it."

"You're out of your damn mind. Your *turn*? I'm a human being, for Pete's sake. You don't get a *turn* with me. That's not how this works. Where is my cat? Do you even know?"

He shook his head. "If you knew the things I've done for you, you wouldn't be speaking to me this way—you wouldn't dare. I let that stupid little cat out to get you to come out here and talk to me just in case the wine and flowers didn't work. Just like I did at your birthday party all those years ago. Don't you see the lengths I would go to for you? How lucky you are to have me in your life?"

Red clouded my vision as I tried to comprehend what he had just said. "You stole my cat? Persephone? You took her? And Cheddar?"

I saw—as if I were in another body—my fist lash out and hit him in the face. He stumbled back but didn't fall.

His eyes flashed with anger as he rubbed his cheek. "I

would have given her back if you had given me even the slightest hint that you wanted to go out with me. But all you did was cry over that stupid animal. It was hardly worth it."

"Where is Cheddar?!" I screamed.

He shrugged. "Around the store somewhere, I assume. I left the doors open. I put him in your herb garden. He'll find his way inside. He should be fine."

"He's a baby! And so was Persephone. How could you do that?"

"Persephone was fine, and she had a good life. I hid her in my car and gave her to my cousin in Washington as a birthday present. Calm down."

"*Calm down?* This is my life you're fucking with! How dare you?!"

"Because it's MY TURN, damn you!" He thumped a fist against his chest. "I'm a catch, Holly. Why can't you see that when everyone else does. Everyone wants me. I can have any woman in Sweetbriar, and I chose you. I've been choosing you since we were kids and you've always been too damn blind to see it."

"And I've been telling you since we were kids that I don't like you like that. How is it my fault that you don't know how to fucking listen!" I shrieked. "No means no, goddamn it!"

I turned to leave but he grabbed me by the arms and shook me before I could get away. Up close I could see his eyes were red rimmed and lit up with manic energy.

"I saw you!" he yelled. "I saw you and now it's all I can see."

"You're fucking crazy. Maren was right about you. I want you out of here. Go away and never come back. Let go of me."

"I saw you. I saw you, Holly." Tears streamed down his face, and he swiped them clumsily away with his sleeve.

"You saw me? What the hell are you talking about?" I tried to pull out of his grip, but he held me too tight.

"I saw you in his truck, on the side of Petunia Street, sucking him off like you were a common whore. I was parked down the street, but I saw you bend over. I saw how your body moved over his. I know what you were doing to him. How could you debase yourself like that?"

"If you saw me there, then you were following me," I accused as I struggled to get away. "And if you watched it happen, then you are *sick*, Jared." There was no way he just happened to be randomly driving down a deserted, low-traffic street at nearly ten o'clock at night.

He looked away, his nostrils flaring as he seethed in discomfort. "I can forget about what you did with him. I swear I can. But you have to stop acting out like this and accept the fact that you belong to me."

Finally, I was able to wrench my arms out of his grasp. I shoved him and tried to go around him, but he grabbed my upper arm. I shook it off. "Put your hands on me again, Jared, and I'll cut them off."

"Let's discuss this civilly. Can we please do that? Without all the foul language and threats of violence. I'm sorry I grabbed you. I'm sorry I shook you. I shouldn't have done that."

"Fuck. You. The last thing I am feeling right now is civil." I advanced on him, pushing him in the chest as I herded us back in the direction of my shop and back toward safety. "You think you want me? You have no idea what you're asking for, asshole. I do what I want when I want. And if I want to suck my boyfriend's dick in the front seat of his truck on a deserted fucking street, then I'm damn well going to do it. You can't shame me, Jared. Not when you were the pervert following me around and spying on me."

"Watch your mouth!"

"Fuck off!" I shoved him again.

"Stop it." He stumbled backward and I kept shoving. I didn't want to turn my back on him by trying to run away. All I could think about was getting back to my store. Back home. Back to safety.

"I don't know what I'll have to do to get you free of him, but I know I'll think of something. I always do when it comes to you."

"If you even think of hurting Liam, you will deal with me."

I'd pushed him too far. He planted his feet and raised his arm, swinging it to backhand me. I blocked the hit with my forearm and punched him in the stomach.

He stumbled back just as Liam made it to my side, followed by Levi who had Cheddar cradled against his chest.

"You found him!" I cried at the exact moment Liam hauled off and hit Jared square in the jaw. He went flying back to land in the street with a thud. I probably should have attempted to hit him like that, but all I'd been able to think about was getting back to the store. And part of me still underestimated him, which was stupid considering what he had done.

"Oh my god, Levi. Let me see him. Is he okay?" I was desperate to cuddle Cheddar and see for myself he was okay.

"He's fine, Holls. I found him sleeping in your herb garden." Levi's eyes were gentle as they met mine. "Take a deep breath. It's going to be okay. Mom and Gram are with Jude back at the store. Why did you come all the way over here? I saw you under the streetlamp when I was heading back inside."

I glared at Jared. "He called me over. Told me he spotted Cheddar. I wasn't thinking."

I took Cheddar from Levi and held him to my face, kissing his tiny pink nose. "He smells like basil." A hysterical laugh shot out of me at the same time I burst into tears and clutched him to my throat. I hiccupped out another sob. "He took Persephone, Levi. He took her from my birthday party and gave her away."

"The fuck?" Levi spun toward Jared. "You motherfucker," he ground out. "Don't you fucking move."

Liam drew me into his arms.

Levi took his cell from his back pocket. "I'm calling 911. He needs to be arrested. We need this to be on record. He hurt you, Holly. Look at your arms." I glanced down and saw purple bruises starting to form all over my upper arms.

"What's going on?" Jared stirred on the ground, rubbing his chin as he sat up.

"You're going to jail," Levi snapped. "That's what's going on, asshole." But Jared had stopped listening.

"Get your hands off her," he spat at Liam. "I've known her longer than you. I've earned the right to have her. How long have you been here? Not even a year."

"Shut your fucking mouth. Holly has been through enough. If you were any kind of man, you would understand that. If you actually cared about her, you would have never treated her like this. Levi, take her inside, She doesn't need to hear any more of his shit."

"No, I won't leave you out here, Liam. You've been through enough too."

"Come on, Holly," Levi took my hand to pull me along with him. "Cops are on their way."

"Not without Liam."

"What we've been through is not the same, Holly," Liam's voice was gentle as he urged me to go with Levi. "Not nearly. Go inside with your brother. I'll make sure he doesn't go anywhere while we wait for the police. That's it, okay?"

"The police?" Jared scoffed. "What would we possibly need them for?" He stood and brushed himself off.

"To arrest your stupid ass, Jared," I shot out. "Think about it." I could see him becoming aware of how far over the line he had gone. Maybe he was sobering up.

"Stay right there," Liam growled. "If you run, I will

chase you. And I promise you won't like what happens after that."

I realized Liam needed to see this through to the end more than I did. He was a protector. It was part of his nature. If I didn't let him take charge here, he'd feel like he failed me, and I couldn't allow that to happen again. So I followed Levi into the house and watched through the windows as a squad car pulled up to arrest Jared.

Chapter 24
Two Months Later

Liam

The first few weeks after Jared's arrest were rough. It sent Holly back into the fear cycle she'd been lost in when she came back to Sweetbriar. We had slept with the lights on, and she barely left my side.

But between therapy, talking things through with me and Cade, and Luke and I taking her out to Jed's to join our PTSD group, she was on the mend once again.

And as for Jared, it was unlikely he'd do any time, but he appeared to be properly chagrined now that everyone in town had found out what he had been up to all these years. Between his humiliation, his horrified and apologetic mother, and the restraining order, it was doubtful he'd ever get near Holly again. And if he did, he'd have me to deal with. Not to mention, Holly herself. Once the fear started to dissipate it was replaced with a profound amount of anger.

But now we were back to where we were. We'd earned the right to the peace we'd found together, and I was about to make it permanent.

Dinner was waiting for me on the table when I arrived at Holly's shop after closing time. And I knew I was in for a treat.

Occasionally, Holly would greet me at the door wearing an apron and not much else. She called it living out her 'wifey' fantasy.

Meatloaf and mashed potatoes were always on the menu for wifey night, with snickerdoodles for dessert. It was the only thing she could cook, and it was my favorite.

"Honey, I'm home," I called, playing along.

"Hello, dear," she drawled as she popped out of the kitchen clad in an apron that said, "Kiss the cook" with lacy yellow lingerie peeking out from the sides. I couldn't wait to see it, but I had an agenda tonight.

She was about to get a whole lot more than a kiss.

She didn't know it, but I was about to make this little game we sometimes played together a reality.

Forget moving in together. We were past that now.

I wanted to marry her.

"Sit down."

She pouted. "But I wanted to—"

"Let's make this game real. What do you think?"

Without a word, she sat at the tea shop table she had set up for our dinner.

I crossed through the store and got down on a knee.

Holly gasped, her right hand flying to cover her mouth. "Oh my god. Liam, please make this real."

I glanced at her left hand daintily sitting in her lap.

She lifted it, waggling her fingers with a huge grin plastered to her gorgeous face as I pulled the ring box from my pocket and opened it.

I wanted to explain. "It's a canary diamond—"

"Oh, Liam, it's beautiful! And with all those tiny diamonds around it, it looks just like the sun."

"Exactly. Will you marry me, sunshine?"

"Yes." She slid out of the chair and into my arms, kissing me all over as tears ran down her face and she held me tight. "I don't know how to be this happy, but I can't wait to figure it out with you."

Epilogue

Summer
Holly

It was my wedding day.

My sisters surrounded me as I took one last look at myself in the mirror before I headed out to marry Liam. "You are stunning, darling," my mother whispered from the doorway, Gram at her side.

"You're beautiful, Hollyberry." Gram brushed a tear from her cheek and echoed the sentiment.

I was wearing yard after yard of white lace and chiffon, and with the corseted bodice and poofy off-the-shoulder sleeves, I looked like a sexy boho cloud. My sisters were dressed in pale hues of yellow silk and carrying bouquets of white roses tied with yellow ribbon. They looked like sunbeams.

Baby's breath and yellow flowers of every type decorated the entire property. I'd been determined to have my wedding feel bright and full of sun even if the sky above was dark and hazy with rain. Because in Sweetbriar, Oregon, you could never predict how the weather would be, even in the summertime.

After she had the twins, Lily decided her next project would be my wedding. She had insisted on sparing no expense when it came to marrying off her "little brother" and as such, she had gone so far overboard that everywhere I turned, I gasped at the beauty that met my eye.

She had heard Liam call me sunshine at the Sunday dinner after he proposed, took one look at my ring, and freaked out. "Let me plan your wedding!" she had shrieked.

And I said okay, with zero clue of what I would be getting myself into. After my permission had been granted, she and Rose had exchanged a look then left mid-dinner to run down to my mom's office to create a shared Pinterest board for their ideas.

I had envisioned something small, maybe a trip to Las Vegas. Or a dinner with family at my parent's house, or perhaps in my garden at home.

But no.

This was an extravaganza.

And I had to admit . . .I freaking loved it.

My entire family was here, waiting in the same barn where Rose and Trevor had gotten married back on New Year's Eve. But instead of midnight, it was midday, and instead of a small affair contained to the barn, my wedding had spilled everywhere.

"It's time," my father informed us.

Lily, Rose, and Violet followed Mom and Gram out while my father waited for me in the doorway. "Are you ready, honey?"

"Yes. I've never been as ready for anything as I am for this. I can't wait."

"I'm happy for you. Liam fits into this family like he was born into it." Humor crossed his face. "But I guess it's lucky for you that he wasn't."

I shook my head and took his arm. "Right? Let's go."

As we walked the gravel pathway to the barn, I held my dad's arm and marveled at how far I had come since I'd returned home. At how far this entire family had come. My sisters were all married and happy. Cade and Charlotte were back together; now it was time for Jude, Levi and Ash to find their own piece of happiness. I had no doubt they would now that they had four sisters drunk on happily-ever-after and waiting to meddle in their lives.

"I am so happy, Dad. I could fly down to the barn."

He squeezed me to him in a hug. "I'm so proud of you, Holly. You've lived a huge life and you're barely thirty. And now you're going to share it with one of the best men I've ever met. Liam will make you even happier, of that I have no doubt."

I brushed a tear from my cheek as we approached the barn. The doors were thrown wide and trimmed in flowers and fluffy tulle ribbon wound with shimmery lights. The aisle was liberally strewn with yellow and white rose petals. I stopped at the head next to my sisters as the music began and watched them go one by one,

At the end of the aisle stood Liam with Luke and my brothers at his side.

"I love you," he mouthed when he spotted me.

"Come on." I gave my dad's arm a tug and he laughed when I rushed us, kicking up rose petals all the way until I reached Liam and he took my hand.

"I love you too," I whispered. "Let's make this real."

I hope you enjoyed Heart to Heart!
Scan the QR code for *Sunshine Hearts*, a Liam
and Holly bonus scene!

About the Author

Nora Everly is a lifelong bookworm. She started reading the good stuff once she grew tall enough to sneak the romance novels off the top of her mother's bookshelf and it has been non-stop ever since.
Once upon a time she was a substitute teacher and an educational assistant. Now she's a writer and stay at home mom to two small humans and one fat cat.
Nora lives in the Pacific Northwest with her family and her overactive imagination.

Find her at noraeverly.com